Glorified, Resurrected
and
His Kingdom is HERE !

Diane Cordaire!

INTRODUCTION

This book allowed me to clarify a vision that was too deep for me to reach. We can have words like glorification, resurrection, and 'Thy Kingdom Come', but those words need to turn into a reality within oneself, otherwise, they are just words with no power. I've noticed with each book I write, a new light shines within my very being, enabling me to walk towards the completion of my existence on earth. This book, I hope, will bring that light to others in the Glorification awareness, resurrection, and God's Kingdom here on earth.

Years of seeking the Lord and following Him have propelled me up the Holy Mountain to expect Christ's image to be seen in human existence. *When You said, "Seek My face," My heart said to You, 'Your face, LORD, I will seek'* [Psalm 27:8]. Many individuals throughout history have attained this higher calling. Moses, Elijah, Elisha, Enoch, and Jesus Christ are some to mention. Elijah and Enoch left earth without tasting death, and Moses' body was never found. Jesus Christ was transfigured, and then a week later He went further and was resurrected to walk the earth. These two processes are different!

The transfiguration and reappearance of Christ are part of us all! But not all will walk upon the earth in this glorified state. During an allotment of time, I have followed Jesus Christ in the fellowship of suffering through the cross. It led me to the tomb of aloneness! My walk with Him is taking me further up the Holy Mountain of my soul to see His face. When you look at His face, you will experience glory. But it's only when we have faith to see His reign upon the earth that we can become co heirs of His Glory. This will make us an expression of the same glory. God created the earth and all that is in it! The Father of heaven and earth spoke each one of us into existence with His plan engraved on our DNA. *All flesh is mortal, but the righteous are immortal and divine.*

I hope to fulfil His call to reveal His glory within this earthen vessel. *Many are called, few are chosen are the words from our Lord* [Matthew 22:14]. It is an honour and a privilege to be elected. *For we are His workmanship, created in Christ Jesus for good works, which God prepared beforehand that we should walk in them* [Ephesians 2:10]. God anointed and marked us for this mission of mercy upon the earth. These last days will require a people who are glorified in Christ's image. The mission is to bring multitudes into "The Kingdom of God" harvest. The time is now for a new reign of Christ upon the earth.

My research includes *writings of Kenneth Visscher:*
overcomers.ca
- Kept by His Gaze
- The Prophecy of Sounding the Alarm
- Flesh of His Flesh
- Addendum 1-6
- The New Jerusalem

CHAPTER 1

Understanding our Existence

We take our existence for granted most of the time. We never really think tomorrow won't show up because it always seems to arrive. With a new sunrise and a burst of light, we call it 'today'. I've often thought living on earth is like having an incredible force field around my life holding me on earth. Most people don't even notice; they just live out their days in busyness. Our days, if not yet converted into His Grace, will have death at the helm! It's our diminished physical nature and mind that has taken over without us even noticing. To live differently takes awareness and a new confession of direction. The alternative part of our decayed carnal nature is a perfect interpretation and expression of ourselves. But is it us, or is it the reflection of our Creator? Recognising our fallen nature so we can pass through to perfection is the art of life. Having another vision past death is "Thy Kingdom Come". When Christ makes Himself known, it's not long before we stand on the battleground of our own carnal nature. However, we soon see Christ steering the ship towards improved horizons. With life at the helm, *Death has no sting* [I Corinthians 15:55].

Faith will get you there under the banner of restored, resurrected life!

To begin! Knowledge is for those who call for it. *If you truly call out to insight and lift your voice to understanding, if you seek it like silver and search it out like hidden treasure* [Proverbs 2:4]. Once you have gained knowledge, we sail over to the experience by faith. Depending on who you are, healing accompanies the experience. When healed, this knowledge and experience develop into wisdom, and new freedoms emerge through our soul. This new freedom will show up in our natural realm; hence new light springs forth from your being.

If this passage from knowledge to experience and healing does not develop, we stay in knowledge. Or, as I call it, intelligence held up by pride! This can develop into religion and lead to death in the body. I met a fellow who moved away from God's presence because he went into the slipstream of His own intelligence. When I listen to him, the knowledge he sprouts comes from TV or books. He takes pride in his knowledge! A hurt person who has walked away from the presence of God will use pride as his elevator. You can see that a person like him is decaying from the inside out and is an empty vessel.

Pride will fall along with all understandings that is built on man's pride!

Resurrected life is where we were created to be before we walked away. God's expression through your life is perfect! We need to make our way home into the perfection of His expression. *Therefore, you shall be perfect, just as your Father in heaven is perfect* [Matthew 5:48].

Many individuals forsake Our Lord Jesus Christ by leaving Him out of the equation. Or by going straight to the Father with their requests. Acknowledging Jesus Christ as Lord and Messiah has been told. *Our Lord says, I am the way, the truth, and the life: no man comes unto the Father, but by me* [John 14:6]. Operating outside the instructions of the Holy scriptures is not acknowledging the Father's Son nor acknowledging the

Father's request. Humanity has robbed the Holy scriptures by putting them into their own understanding or religions. There are many deviations today. I believe in the last calculation, there were 60,000 denominations with different names. To add further, you have New Age, Buddhism, Hinduism and every other type of 'ism' known to man. Man has gone his own way and understanding to stand at the edge of his own fall. *All we, like sheep, have gone astray; We have turned, everyone, to his own way* [Isaiah 53:6].

Every society ends! But with an end, there are continually new beginnings. It is written through the Holy scriptures *that Christ will return and every eye shall see him and every knee shall bow* [Rev 1:7]. *No one knows the day or hour, not even the angels in heaven, nor the Son, but only the Father. As it was in the days of Noah, so will it be at the coming of the Son of Man. For in the days before the flood, people were eating and drinking, marrying and given in marriage, up to the day Noah entered the ark* [Matthew 24:36-38].

When the time arrives, many will miss the day and hour of the coming of the Lord! Because their focus will still be on their own desires or their battles within their minds. Or they will sit on their personal knowledge and understanding! *Trust in the LORD with all your heart, and lean not on your own understanding* [Proverbs 3:5]. The Lord plans to glorify the righteous who have overcome and allow them to reign with Him upon the earth. *You have made them to be a kingdom and priests to serve our God, and they will reign on the earth* [Revelation 5:10]. Who are the righteous? Many religions claim they are these people! What I've seen is many of these people are in knowledge of the scriptures and that knowledge has never converted to righteousness. When the Lord calls His chosen people, He will take one from there and one from there! He is after the heart of man, not His works. The Lord does not care if you go to church or call yourself by a religious name. God doesn't care how much money is in your sacks or how many properties you own! He will glorify His people wherever they are and whoever they are.

The coming glorification is for those who have won crowns. The first crown is for running the race! *Do you not know that in a race all the runners run, but only one receives the prize? So, run that you may obtain* it [1 Corinthians 9:24]. The next crown is of joy. We receive this crown for overcoming and healing. *For you are our hope, our joy, and the crown when our Lord Jesus Christ comes* [1Thesalionians]. The third crown is of righteousness for becoming holy. *Now there is in store for me the crown of righteousness, which the Lord, the righteous Judge, will award to me on that day—and not only to me but also to all who have longed for his appearing* [2 Timothy 4:8]. The fourth crown is of Glory, *and when the Chief Shepherd appears, you will receive the crown of glory that does not fade away* [1 Peter 5:4]. And lastly, the crown of life. *Blessed is a man who perseveres under trial; for once he has been approved, he will receive the crown of life* [James 1:12].

What crowns have you been granted? If you haven't received a crown or you didn't realise you needed a crown, a friendly suggestion is to look at where you got diverted away from running the race and start running.

The glorification is the image of Christ in earthy bodies – heavenly bodies walking here on earth! *Arise, shine, for your light has come and the glory of the Lord is upon you. See, darkness is over the earth and thick darkness is over the people, but the Lord rises upon you and His glory is over you. Nations will come to your light and Kings to your dawn* [Isaiah 60:1]. That is my favourite verse in the Bible! Without that verse, I wouldn't be the person I am today. It has given me hope throughout the seasons to seek the face of the one who is Glory. To develop a pure heart, mind and body has been my endeavour. I have more crowns to receive, and the next crown is Glory!

For we know that the whole creation groans and labours with birth pangs together until now. Not only that, but we also who have the first fruits of the Spirit, even we ourselves groan within ourselves, eagerly waiting for the adoption, the redemption of our body [Romans 8:22].

Recognising our true image is in Him, not ourselves, is a key! *To them God willed to make known what are the riches of the glory of this mystery among the Gentiles: which is Christ in you, the hope of glory* [Colossians 1:27]. Stepping out in genuine faith, expecting the quickening of His Spirit to come and glorify our mortal bodies, is our cry. *But if the Spirit of Him that raised up Jesus from the dead dwells in you, He that raised up Christ from the dead shall also quicken your mortal bodies by His Spirit that dwells in you* [Romans 8:11]. Offer our bodies is a living sacrifice holy and pleasing. *This is your true worship* [Romans 12:1]. This offering was the last offering Jesus Christ did upon the cross.

Remember, His mission was to show us the way! We are attached to a body, spirit, and soul. *Remember him—before the silver cord is severed and the golden bowl is broken; before the pitcher is shattered at the spring, and the wheel broken at the well, and the dust returns to the ground it came from, and the spirit returns to God who gave it* [Ecclesiastes 12: 4-7]. This silver cord is how we are joined spiritually, physically, mentally, and emotionally. Jesus Christ relinquished His spirit, body, and His will as His true worship. This offering discharged carnality (death) and opened the way to receive the resurrected body. Our body, soul, and spirit are a three-cord braid that are not easily broken. This verse speaks of three people operating together to overpower an enemy. Our carnal nature is the enemy! The glorification of Christ's body became the resurrected body walking here on earth. We must give up to go up, as the saying goes. The silver cord is the last stage. Where Christ walked was the last crown. The crown of life, resurrection!

There are two futures near us! Our forefathers and prophets have spoken out in line with Scripture of the coming fall of man and the rise of the Kingdom of God. *And if it seems evil unto you to serve the LORD, choose you this day whom ye will serve; whether the gods which your fathers served that were on the other side of the flood, or the gods of the Amorites, in whose land ye dwell: but as for me and my house, we will serve the LORD"* [Joshua 24:15].

For many years, I have listened to people, regardless of their religious status, saying they are just waiting for the Lord's return. This has played in my ears! I thought it would happen differently from the way they describe the return. The way it's expressed fobs off the burden from them being part of the coming Kingdom. They are waiting to be taken away in the clouds. They are waiting for the wrong thing! They're not in the right place to sit in high places and rule this earth with the King of Glory. *You ask and do not receive, because you ask amiss, that you may spend it on your pleasures* [James 4:3].

People who have overcome will bring the Kingdom onto the earth. The tribulation the worldly people are going through with the downfall of the schemes of man will look as though they are going forward, but in reality, they are not. As the tribulation continues many people are rising who have identified themselves with Zion, the Holy City. That City lives within their very being. *The kingdom of God is within you* [Luke 17:21]. They recognise who they are and the purposes and the intentions of our Lord here on earth. These people know that the Lord God is in control, not man's mind and schemes. The world is on the broad road that leads to destruction. *For wide is the gate and broad is the road that leads to destruction, and many enter through it. But small is the gate and narrow the road that leads to life, and only a few find it* [Matthew 7:13]. Jesus clarifies that we all stand at a spiritual crossroads, and there are two paths in front of us. *This day I call the heavens and the earth as witnesses against you that I have set before you life and death, blessings and curses. Now choose life, so that you and your children may live* [Deuteronomy 30:19].

There will be an outpouring of the Holy Spirit in the last days. The Lord's plan is that no man should perish, so He will go to great lengths to get people into their right heart and mind before His return.

This will be the second time in history there will be an outpouring. The first was at Pentecost, where fire came upon the hundred and twenty in the upper room. That hundred and twenty turned into billions of people who have made a commitment to the Lord over time or have heard about our

Lord Jesus Christ. And all of that started with Christ and His twelve disciples.

That's multiplication at its best!

The harvest of people will be the greatest ever seen in the history upon humanity. Before catastrophe takes place upon the earth, this final outpouring of the Holy Spirit will be seen on all mankind. *All nations, great and small, will experience the Lord. In the last days, God says, I will pour out my Spirit on all people. Your sons and daughters will prophesy, your young men will see visions, your old men will dream dreams* [Acts 2:17]. All of humanity! Are you ready?

I had a vision:

I was standing on the edge of a mountain with a friend who has walked as closely as I have been walking with the Lord. We turned our heads away from the mountain's edge and saw a big rolling cloud encased in the wind coming directly at us. My friend said, turn and go with it! As we turned, the cloud picked us up, and we were off the mountain's edge, riding the front of the cloud. I looked along the cloud, and only a few people were on this cloud and they were a long way away from where I was with my friend. The cloud was dropping over everyone on the planet. Everybody was coming out of their shops and businesses and homes looking up as the cloud came over them. It was coming over their minds and changing them. I was then dropped into a dirty quarry with a metal box. Inside the box were all the things that I would need to help release the people. As I looked up, there was a dirty brick building in the quarry. Behind the dirty glass on the building, multitudes of people with their faces and hands on the windows calling to let them out. I then looked back over at the world to see what had happened. Most people didn't return to their businesses or houses. They changed direction to go with the Lord! But some did return to do the same thing as they were doing before the cloud came over them. They ignored the outpouring.

....

The harvest of souls needs to return to their original destination, Zion. I hear preachers talk of revival, but they don't think big enough. It will be an outpouring over all the earth! And no man will say they carried this outpouring of the Holy Spirit. *I am the LORD, that is My name; And My glory I will not give to another, Nor My praise to carved images* [Isaiah 42:8]. When it's the Lord's glory, no man can take credit! In past revivals we hear people saying! *'There he is!'* or *'Here he is!' Do not go running off after them* [Luke 17:23].

Where is Zion? Once again, I've heard many preachers speak of Zion as bricks and mortar. Zion lives within our very being! It's a place within our spirit. It's the Holy Mountain where the Lord lives in us. Zion was always home! We became foggy and couldn't see where home was. Nor could we remember because our soul became polluted by the world. We got stuck living in our caves or homes and thinking that is home. Or church congregations have said they are home. It isn't! The city of our Lord, Zion, is within and home is there. We were diverted away from the gates of Zion through the distractions of the world. And we forgot we had some place else to be because we purchased the story of death and the world.

This latter-day outpouring of the Holy Spirit will draw individuals out of their caves or homes back on the journey to Zion, the Holy City of our Lord. Our pilgrimage to Zion is conquering the world! The world is thoughts, flesh, ears, and eyes cleansed and given as an offering to Our Lord. I wrote a book, which I never produced called 'Political Correctness is a False god'. That book separated man's mind from God's mind. The journey is overcoming and coming out of the world back into holiness. In a politically correct world, I could not say 'man's mind'. I do not belong to that thought or the world.

Zion is a people who entered the Holy of Holies within themselves. They have overcome their darkened, compromised soul. Overcoming the world brings more of Christ's character alive in you, and this shines in the darkened world. We are living stones, and Christ is the cornerstone. So, this is what the sovereign Lord says: *See, I lay a stone in Zion, a tested stone, a precious cornerstone for a sure foundation; the one who trusts will never be dismayed. I will make justice the measuring line and righteousness the plumb line* [Isaiah 28:16]. He has built His church upon this stone. The church is a people, not a building or an organisation with a name on it. When the time is right, signs and wonders will follow this revelation because Christ has found His dwelling place upon the earth, YOU. The overcomers know who they serve, the King of Glory. And they will display His Glory and power in these latter days.

The 'Righteous' will be presented with new gifts from the Lord in healing and miracles, and they will be His signs and wonders upon the earth. Their part in the Kingdom is to release people from their self-imposed prisons and heal the sick. Also, they have tools to help people overcome. These chosen people will display His Glory. *Arise, shine; For your light has come! And the glory of the LORD is risen upon you* [Isaiah 60:1]. The elected have been given permission to enter the gates of righteousness because the Lord has found no spot of blemish in them. *That He might present to Himself the church in all her glory, having no spot or wrinkle or any such thing; but that she would be holy and blameless* [Ephesians 5:27]. There are seven churches in the last days. The Lord has nothing against only two of those churches. One of those being the overcomers - the other is the martyrs. Not all the seven churches will be presented to the Lord as his bride.

Individuals who haven't reached holiness will have opportunities set out before them to pick up the veil and follow the Lord. *Blessed are those who wash their robes, so that they may have the right to the tree of life and may enter the city by its gates. Outside the city are the dogs—the sorcerers, the sexually immoral, the murderers, the idol worshipers, and all who love to live a lie* [Rev 22:15]. These camps of sorcerers, sexual immoral, murders, idol worshipers live in our nations or our soul. Overcoming all darkness and becoming pure of heart causes us to enter the gates of our Lord's City! *And I John saw the holy city, new Jerusalem, coming down from God out of heaven, prepared as a bride adorned for her husband* [Rev 21:2].

Open the gates, that the righteous nation which keeps the faith may enter in [Isaiah 26:1]. These gates are Zion the Holy City. The Kingdom that lives in you and me.

The Kingdom of God is so far removed from what we live in nowadays. Our world is like an old garment or old wineskin, running on death fumes. *And no one puts new wine into old wineskins; or else the new wine bursts the wineskins, the wine is spilled, and the wineskins are ruined* [Mark 2:22]. New wineskins must contain new wine. The Kingdom is glorious, and all who are inside the gates have the same presence, which is the Lord's presence. It is a place where rivers of living water flow. These rivers are in you. The righteous operate outside the parameters of their mind. They are taught to walk in the spirit and have the same powers as the spirit of God. They are anointed by God!

I had an encounter of operating outside my thinking to watch what the Lord did in a situation that required heavenly help. I didn't know the answer to the dilemma! The answer was revealed by the Spirit. I knew it wasn't me because it wasn't something I would do. It was the Spirit of God operating through me. The situation was resolved, and I walked away. It left mouths a gasp as they had just witnessed the supernatural in progress. *The Lord says however, as it is written: "What no eye has seen, what no ear has heard, and what no human mind has conceived" — the things God has prepared for those who love him* [1 Corinthians 2:9]. That happened to me! I hadn't seen nor had I ever conceived, and I hadn't heard of what moved through me by the Spirit of the living God. When I sauntered away from the situation, I was flabbergasted. It made me say to the Lord, "Oh we have seen nothing yet." Take me into Zion through the gates of righteousness within the Holy gates so I can be part of the great outpouring of the Holy Spirit. To rule this earth with you was my request to the Lord.

The rule of man has failed upon the earth. There are no more chances for man to get it right. In these last days, tribulation will come upon humanity like we have never seen before. *The*

Lord said when we see wars and rumours of wars, don't be concerned. When we see floods and earthquakes, that is just the beginning of birth pangs. Man is creating famines by causing supplies to be held up. This is in alignment with the son of perdition being revealed. Don't be hoodwinked by what they report. *For that day will not come until there is a great rebellion against God and the man of lawlessness is revealed—the one who brings destruction* [2 Thessalonians 2:3]. Who is the son of Perdition? He is being prepared secretly, and he will claim he is god. If you cause unrest and instability, then it's easy for humanity to be submissive to a new rule. This new rule will bring peace and stability for a time. This is calm before the storm theory! *While people are saying, 'Peace and safety,' destruction will come on them suddenly, as labour pains on a pregnant woman, and they will not escape* [1 Thessalonians 1:3].

This developing destruction that's going to take place on the earth is something out of movies I've watched. Rocks falling from heaven, rivers poisoned. A third of the creatures in the sea destroyed. A third of the ships disappear, and people are killed. Plagues, famines, and much more! And humanity brought it on themselves by going their own way. They who have washed their robes, meaning overcoming the world, will go through the tribulation, but the Lord will shorten those days because of His elect. *And except those days should be shortened, there should no flesh be saved: but for the elect's sake those days shall be shortened* [Matthew 24:22].

The tribulation is ridding the earth of wickedness. *The righteous shall never be removed: but the wicked shall not inhabit the earth* [Proverb 10:30]. This is the righteous inheritance to be coheirs of the earth and reign with Our Lord Jesus Christ.

This new reign has begun 'Thy Kingdom upon the earth' Halleluiah! Long time coming, but it's here. UNDER NEW MANAGMENT 'Kingdom management'.

CHAPTER 2

The Kingdom is Here

The Kingdom age is moving upon the earth!

You may not perceive this Kingdom because you are still battling your own land within your soul, that's tribulation. The righteous have been interceding, prophesying, praying, and walking out in their walk the call of 'Thy Kingdom Come'. God set them aside. They've been calling in the Glory and His Kingdom to the earth. Nobody knows who they are because it hasn't been necessary to know them. The righteous will be in the tribulation, but will not be touched by the tribulation. God has already judged the true church first. *Judgement must begin at the household of God. and if it begins with us, what will be the outcome for those who do not obey the gospel of God?* [1Peter 4:17].

The true church has already overcome and is standing in alignment with the King of Glory. They can see the tribulation but can't feel the tribulation in their life. They've become the living stones of the Lord's temple upon the earth, and they stand upon the rock of the cornerstone. *As you come to him, the living Stone—rejected by humans but chosen by God and precious to him, you also, like living stones, are being built into a spiritual house to be a holy priesthood, offering spiritual sacrifices acceptable to God through Jesus Christ. For in Scripture it says: See, I lay a stone in Zion, a chosen and precious cornerstone, and I will never put the one who trusts in him to shame* [1 Peter 2:4-6].

Righteous and just people are one of the same people. Righteousness means free from guilt or sin. A Just person means behaving with what is morally right and fair. A belief in Jesus Christ and a form of godliness isn't enough. You will be put through the fire of God the same as all humanity in the tribulation. There is only one plan. To establish the Lord's kingdom on the earth. To see everything restored. Restitution of all things!

This age will display His Glory on a people on the earth. The transformed, glorified church is not a religion, a doctrine, or a society of individuals who declared a belief in Jesus Christ. The transformed, glorified church is those who have overcome just as Jesus overcame. The souls of these people were brought under the fire of God, which created sanctification. Their Lord has set out the path for those who wanted to follow Him. The followers set their faces as flint as they pressed on for the goal of seeing Him 'face to face' to behold His Glory. Their focus was not on what they could do in ministry or the efforts they produced upon the earth. *They were faithful in the small so they can be trusted with the more. Whoever can be trusted with very little can also be trusted with much, and whoever is dishonest with very little will also be dishonest with much* [Luke 16:10]. These people knew who their life belonged to. It was not their own. Their life belonged to the King of Glory. The overcomers, as they have been identified, have left their earthly havens to follow their Lord and saviour. When they left their homes, they also left their identity and possessions. *Forgetting what is behind and straining toward what is ahead, I press toward the mark for the prize of the high calling of God in Christ Jesus* [Philippians 3 :14].

It takes a long time to re-identify completely with the Spirit of God. We have had a lifetime of identifying with the flesh and natural realm. The process of re-identifying with another way of life is instrumental to the glorification. That's why these people are alone! Others they have known along the way are still identified with the natural realm and flesh or stuck in their religious circuits. They find no communion with them. Not too many people travel this way. *Small is the gate and narrow the road that leads to life, and only few find it* [Matthew 7:14].

This band of overcomers or elect were set aside, and found aloneness is oneness with Christ and oneness is resurrection life. Christ spoke the words that He would arise again. Our Lord is about to rise in all His splendour in His body in His people. The glory set before our eyes is the transformed, glorified life - Christ Himself. Come, for the hour of this call is here. "The time of My appearing is here, all things are now ready, I am the Lord."

Footnote: The Prophecy of Sounding the Alarm by Kenneth Visscher

> *If you have an ear to hear what the*
> *Spirit is saying!*

This age of Kingdom living will declare His glory in His transformed people. Their bodies and lives became a living sacrifice wholly and pleasing. Their gaze, fixed on the King of Glory as they walk this fallen world. They have become the body of Christ upon the earth.

For many years, the religious church has confessed they are the body of Christ. I tested this by gathering many stories and putting them all into a magazine called 'Close Encounters with God'. Most of the people who gave stories came from the building called 'church' and the body of Christ. At the end of this process, I saw that most, not all, of these people were religious people with a story of how they met Jesus Christ. But what was very prominent and stood out was all but a couple were the elect and earmarked to display His Glory in their body. Now with saying that, I believe all people are called the body of Christ, but many are still on their way to that great day when they can be glorified with the greater body upon the earth. It's those who have washed their robes and overcome. The glorified, chosen people are new wine.

The body of Christ is Christ fully alive in a people. They tied their identity to the living God. When you find your identity in Christ, nothing stands in front of His vision. There is always a counterfeit in this Holy walk. What the world speaks is the counterfeit. *Not everyone who says to Me, 'Lord, Lord,' shall enter the kingdom of heaven, but he who does the will of My Father in heaven* [Matthew 7:21].

The small band of overcomers will be glorified on the earth. *And now, Father, glorify me in your presence with the glory I had with you before the world began* [John 17:5].

The body of overcomers will come together for the purpose of their Father. They are Zion, the Holy City. They are living stones, and Jesus Christ is the cornerstone. *You also, like living stones, are being built into a spiritual house to be a holy priesthood, offering spiritual sacrifices acceptable to God through Jesus Christ*

[1Peter 25]. These overcomers having no agenda but to do the will of their Father. Their minds have become Christ's mind and their bodies are being transformed, so when you look upon them, you see they have been with Jesus Christ. They will become His reflection upon the earth. His IMAGE, His TEMPLE, His BRIDE, His KINGDOM.

This company was small, and very finite in number compared to the billions of mankind. But they had now in them the infinite weight of the Lord God Almighty. They were a people who could not perish but through whom the Lord would now pour forth His mighty wonders.

'Flesh of His Flesh' by Kenneth Visscher

There are two gatherings. The small group of people who have overcome are the first to display His Glory. And the second will not happen until the tribulation is at the end. *Immediately after the tribulation of those days, the sun will be darkened, and the moon will not give its light, and the stars will fall from heaven, and the powers of the heavens will be shaken. Then will appear in heaven the sign of the Son of Man, and then all the tribes of the earth will mourn, and they will see the Son of Man coming on the clouds of heaven with power and great glory* [Matthew 24:29].

This next section needs to be read with an open mind, not a religious mind. If you read it with a religious mind, you will miss the keys to your own glorification and the first gathering.

The first blood to cry out from the ground was from Abel. Blood has a voice! The blood of the martyrs cry out from the grave, and the blood of Jesus Christ cries out throughout all creation in earnest expectation waiting for the day of His return. When Jesus Christ was upon the cross, He had the power to lay down His life and to regain His life once again. That power was in Him - that's resurrection power! That same blood gives strength and delivers us from our enemy. It heals the sick and sets the captives free. It is the most powerful weapon in the universe. Redemption, sanctification, and glorification come from the blood of Jesus Christ and delivers us from the power of death. Jesus Christ's blood is God's blood. They share the same blood. The blood has the power to raise people from the dead and cleanse people from demonic forces. His blood restores all things. Christ's blood delivers us from generational curses and the sins of our forefathers. His blood liberates us. Salvation came through the blood shed upon the cross, so no other sacrifice was needed. We can enter the Holy of Holies because of His blood. Sin has no legal claim over our lives because His blood atoned our sins. It restored our blood from the Adamic blood. Jesus Christ paid the debt for your life, and not only did He pay that debt, He recovered all that seemed lost. "It is finished" were His words on that day. Sin has no dominion over us anymore. We are now part of the 'Kingdom of God'. The blood of Jesus Christ eradicated our root and hereditary curses.

For I know the plans I have for you, declares the LORD, plans to prosper you and not to harm you, plans to give you hope and a future [Jeremiah 29:11]. The reason and purpose of who you are belongs to Him. We were created for the creator's plan. Right standing with Him is standing in His plan and future.

I have broken the middle wall of separation between carnal and spirit (flesh), says the Lord. *For I am persuaded, that neither death, nor life, nor angels, nor principalities, nor powers, nor things present, nor things to come, nor height, nor depth, nor any other creature, shall be able to separate us from the love of God, which is in Christ Jesus our Lord* [Romans 8:38]. Christ abolished the enmity that is contained in our fallen nature. One new man stands where there were two! For it pleased the Father that all the fullness should dwell in Jesus Christ. We have this fulness living in us through His blood by His Holy Spirit. You just need to identify with the spirit and blood, not the flesh.

The glorification of the carnal body can be accomplished through the blood of Christ and the overcoming process of flesh. Natural becomes glorified! *And when He had given thanks, He broke the bread, and said, take, eat: this is My body, which is broken for you: do this in remembrance of Me* [1 Corinthians 11:24]. Communion with God is a spiritual doorway. It's beyond your natural understanding and carnal nature. It's by faith you enter! Fasting, prayer, and communion are keys that restore all things. And thanksgiving opens heaven. God has shown us through Scriptures and our forefathers how they lost and won battles. Studying their victories and their downfalls helps to see how the Lord brings and establishes His kingdom through obedient people.

A friend of mine recently said, "I've heard it all before preached to me since I was a little girl." Because of this, she missed the key to the door that opens the way to receive the quickening of the Spirit to be glorified. Religion does that - it numbs you from hearing the truth you're looking for. Many believers have missed the importance of the blood of Jesus. The blood became a cliché; the broken body became a ritual. I had another fellow who manifested when I mentioned the blood of Jesus. He wanted what others wanted - the glorification of the body, but he will miss the mark because the blood is offensive to him. It turns out it is the entry point of everything he ever wanted.

It's those who come through Christ's blood and His body who will stand before the King of Glory. *And now, O Father, glorify Me together with Yourself, with the glory which I had with You before the world was* [John 17:5]. After I prayed these prayers in faith, I stood in oneness with Him.

The Lord will stand upon the earth in full splendour in His earthy tabernacles, the overcomers. This body will be the chosen few, with the Lord as the head. Remember, *many are called few are chosen* [Matthew 22:14]. That's because many will miss the entry point of Jesus Christ and they loved their lives more than Christ's life. *He that loveth his life shall lose it; and he that hated his life in this world shall keep it unto life eternal* [John 12:25]. The weight of God and the power of God will fill people who enter the Glory. They will be as God is! They will only do what the Father tells them.

The harvest of all souls is the purpose of this body of glorified people. This happening will align with the outpouring of the Holy Spirit.

In the last days, God says, I will pour out my Spirit on all people. Your sons and daughters will prophesy, your young men will see visions, your old men will dream dreams [Acts 2:17].

Everything that has been set up against the will of the Father can be brought down. To restore the Kingdom of God back onto the earth as in heaven is the task. This is Zion, the Holy City. This coincides with the thousand-year reign on earth. *Those who share in the first resurrection are holy and blessed. The second death has no power over them, but they will be priests of God and of Christ and will reign with him for a thousand years* [Revelations 20:6]. Is the thousand-year reign after the tribulation, or is it being set up as the tribulation is rolling out in the world? Because I know what the Lord is doing in my life, I know the Kingdom is being set up on earth prophetically as the tribulation is happening. It's a dual existence. Some of us have a call to bring the future into the now. A microcosm, so it can come in a macrocosm. A prophet is someone who sees the future and brings that future to the earth in the NOW. "Thy Kingdom Come".

I will raise up for them a prophet like you from among their fellow Israelites, and I will put my words in his mouth. He will tell them everything I command him. I will call to account anyone who does not listen to my words that the prophet speaks in my name [Deuteronomy 18:18]. So, the prophets served as God's megaphones to declare the will of the Lord in specific regions at specific points in history. But, given the different circumstances they encountered, their authority as God's emissaries often led to additional responsibilities, some good and some bad.

For example, Deborah was a prophet who also served as a political and military leader during the period of the judges when Israel had no king. She was responsible for a substantial military victory over a larger army with superior military technology [Judges 4]. Other prophets helped lead the Israelites during military campaigns, including Elijah [2 Kings 6:8-23]. During the prime points of Israel's history as a nation, the prophets were subtle guides who provided wisdom to God-fearing kings and other leaders. At other times, however, God called prophets to confront the Israelites about idolatry and other forms of sin. They denounced injustice, idolatry, and empty rituals. It was often dangerous to be a prophet. They were unpopular, even persecuted.

The traditional church calls so many people prophets. I question, are all these people prophets? People like the words of the prophets in a church because they are like fortune tellers. True Prophets affect regions, Kings, armies, and the future. The prophets in the church bring words of knowledge to individual people. A different interpretation of prophet!

The revealing of overcomers is felt in the heavenlies through the cry from the grave and the intercessions from Our Lord Jesus Christ. An earnest expectation throughout all creation is waiting for the day to come. *For the creation waits in eager expectation for the children of God to be revealed* [Romans 8:19]. That's a powerful scripture!

The glorified body will display the character and personality of Our Lord Jesus Christ. The Glory is the centre of His being, and it's the centre of our being - if we have overcome our fallen nature and are ready for God to extend His sceptre to quicken our mortal body! *But if the Spirit of him that raised up Jesus from the dead dwell in you, He that raised up Christ from the dead shall also quicken your mortal bodies by His Spirit that dwelleth in you* [Romans 8:11].

We have been made ready! *Arise, shine, for your light has come, and the glory of the LORD rises upon you. See, darkness covers* the earth and thick darkness is over the peoples, but the LORD rises upon you and his glory appears over you. Nations will come to your light, and kings to the brightness of your dawn [Isaiah 60:1]. We will be swallowed up in Him. He doesn't share His Glory because we are made one with him. We become the Glory, but it is Him who is seen. He restores His creation to Himself. I love that! Fully redeemed and restored!

I was staring at the stars in my morning meditation. I watched as the sunlight advanced. It swallowed up the stars, and they became one with creation. The stars' presence faded into the creator's presence. And the two became one! So, the stars still existed, but were swallowed up by the greater existence. That's how it will be when His glory overshadows us. *Waiting for our blessed hope, the appearing of the glory of our great God and Saviour Jesus Christ, He gave Himself for us to redeem us from all lawlessness and to purify for Himself a people for His own possession, zealous for good deeds...* [Titus 2:13-14].

God says He will not share His Glory with another! When we become humble enough, we will know all power, all might, all headship, and everything that was created for Him and through Him belongs to Him. That's when we can enter into full salvation and His righteousness. If we hadn't come to this place, we could not reveal His Glory because our pride would have taken the Glory.

Christ is the spearhead of all things! He is the only one worthy of opening the scrolls in heaven. *Worthy are you, our Lord and God, to receive glory and honour and power, for you created all things, and by your will they existed and were created* [Revelation 4:11]. He is the head of everything and worthy.

We are His body upon the earth. But it's a body of people who aren't religious or full of pride - it's a body that has been purified. Pride has been eliminated, and all iniquities of our forefathers are broken. They have made themselves ready and will reveal the glorified image of Christ upon the earth.

The ark of the covenant, or the ark of His presence, was in my eyes as a presentation of how authentic life should be portrayed. Uzzah, one driver of the cart that carried the ark, put out his hand to steady the ark when it was tipping. It struck him down dead when He touched it! We are putting our hands up on whatever God has given us to do all our lives. We love getting involved and getting our hands all over it. I had an experience recently of not touching the ark and allowing God to do the bringing and the doing. Yes, I still had to sit in the seat and do the things that came my way, but it was His presence that brought the result. It was a simple prayer asking for His blood to cover the tasks and seeing the presence within the ark bring the results. That prayer brought extraordinary results. I had someone who wouldn't usually comment remark how great the results were. If we could learn to do this every day, we would see a different result. The next day I touched the ark, and it was like I was electrocuted, thrown back on my bum. The parameters changed because I didn't adhere to how it was shown to me the previous day.

God wrote the commandments in stone and placed them in an ark. We are the ark, and we carry His presence! Receiving the Holy Spirit is God alive in you. The Scripture: *Abide in me, and I in you. As the branch cannot bear fruit of itself, except it abides in the vine; no more can ye, except ye abide in me. I am the vine; you are the branches: He that abides in me, and I in him, the same brings forth much fruit: for without me you can do nothing* [John 15:4]. Being a spiritual being in a human body is the art to life. We thrust ourselves out into our human natural existence instead of going inward to the spirit. The spirit can bring everything to us under His grace. The spiritual is learnt by seeking God's ways. God is the opposite of what we have been taught in the natural.

Recognising the headship is leading the way and gives permission for the Holy Spirit to set people free. We carry "His Kingdom" within our very being, and if we can't pull down principalities and powers, thus we haven't come far enough to contribute to the coming of the King. Following our Lord isn't consistently clear, but it's our trust and love for Him that propels us forward. When we see individuals set free, darkness is ripped down on this earth. *No weapon forged against you will prevail, and you will refute every tongue that accuses you. This is the heritage of the servants of the Lord, and this is their vindication from me, declares the Lord* [Isaiah 54:17].

We belong to the silent help behind the scenes. And when you know that truth, we have come to where the Spirit of the Lord stands. Champions soar beyond the fire of affliction to be who they are hailed to be, with no fanfare or glory. No pride equals no self-glory! *Therefore, let no one boast in men. For all things are yours* [1 Corinthians 3:21).

Everything is possible, and everything is yours! That is a mighty statement. We are the building blocks bringing 'Thy Kingdom' to the earth. Each of us has this mantle! *So, then you are no longer strangers and aliens, but you are fellow citizens with the saints and members of the household of God, built on* the foundation of the apostles and prophets, Christ Jesus himself being the cornerstone, in whom the whole structure, being joined together, grows into a holy temple in the Lord. In him you also are being built together into a dwelling place for God by the Spirit {Ephesians 19:22).

Recently I have been connecting to the prophets and apostles, our forefathers. Recognising their good and faithful work. Jesus Christ has been my cornerstone, but I have felt this connection growing with an appreciation of what our forefathers have done for us. They are not just Bible stories! They are people who watch as a cloud of witnesses, cheering us on as we finish the work that they started.

Individuals live to die instead of realising that resurrection is higher than death. *O death, where is thy sting? O grave, where is thy victory?* [1Corinthians 15:55] Jesus Christ went through death and rose again in resurrection power. Christ lived in this state on earth. That's how it should be for us! It's a shift of mindset to know you are resurrected for life and not for death. You are also royalty, as Jesus Christ is King. If death has been taken out of us, resurrection and immortality are our promises to replace our carnal nature. It takes years for the potter to reshape the clay vessel, which is us. *But now, O LORD, You are our Father; We are the clay, and You are our potter; And all we are the work of Your hand* [Isaiah 64:8]. It also takes time to take the dross off our life, which leaves the silver. *Take away the dross from the silver, and the smith has material for a vessel; take away the wicked from the presence of the king and his throne will be established in righteousness* [Proverbs 25:4-5). Silver, in my understanding, is His Glory! They say when a silversmith takes away the dross from the silver, it is heat that separates them. The dross is scooped off, which leaves the silver. Ask a silversmith when do you know you have all the dross? His answer is, "When you can see your reflection in the silver." Glory is the Holy Spirit at the centre of our being and we are His reflection if you allow the fire of God to burn away the dross.

That they all may be one; as the Father, is in me, and I in Him, that they also may be one in us: that the world may believe that you have sent me. And the glory which you gave to me I have given them; that they may be one, even as we are one. I in them, and you in me, that they may be made perfect in one; and that the world may know that you have sent me, and has loved them, as you have loved me [John 17: 21-23].

This generation will see the Lord receive His place on the earth. *Behold, He comes with clouds; and every eye shall see Him* [Revelation 1:7]. *He is the sure foundation which we have built upon. In Him we will be joined together to become the complete building and rise to become the holy temple in the Lord* [Ephesians 2:19-21]. Zion, the Holy Temple, the body of Christ, the transformed overcomers joined to become Zion, the Holy city on earth. Glorified! To take part in Zion is to rise up above the mortal sphere. Beyond death, hunger, sickness and pain is the realm we are talking about. These chosen few believe all things are possible! They believe the resurrection power will transcend them into His likeness. Enoch transcended and so did Elijah. Jesus Christ showed us it is possible to walk in the resurrection power and be on earth in this transformed eternal body. This is the journey of an overcomer! They have followed the path of their risen Lord into resurrection so they can appear in righteousness with Him when He touches them with His Glory.

This next writing is a vision given to Kenneth Visscher regarding the transformation of the overcomers [overcomers.ca].

"The transformation of these people will come as a swirling mass of Glory proceeding from the midst of the bones outward through the cell structure and organs of the body of these chosen people. The sword of the Lord, even by the tip of the sword then cleaved apart one side of the larger bone revealing inside it the mass of marrow and the formation of blood. As the Lord's sword had cleaved this apart the marrow became fully visible, so also the formation of the blood, which was created with the Mystery of Iniquity fully rampant within it. Down deep in the marrow were the platelets of red blood, each based on this earthly body and created as one with the blood of the world since the time of Adam, even until this day. Their bodies were plagued by being subject to death, was then changed cell by cell in a moment of time, a "flash" of existence, from one earthly clay body now to an earthly clay body filled with the swirling mass of the glory of the Lord. As the glory moved through the cell structure each cell became brand new, each one in order, from the inside out to the very skin upon the body. The clay structure of the person as to their features and as to their person remained the same, but they entered now a deathless state. A state of existence yet in clay, but in clay that cannot return to dust. Clay that cannot be burned with the fires of man. Clay that cannot be harmed by the evil council of men who would war against the purposes of the Lord in making all things new. As the mortal clay was changed to immortal clay, and as the corruptible clay was changed to incorruptible clay, so then the person entered the eternal glorified state, filled with the weight of God and the power of God with no restriction as to His mass or power or glory. The Lord in infinite holiness now possessed the cells and the clay of the vessel He had chosen. They were changed from the natural body to a body now a glorified body. For the

swirling mass that came forth in such a manner was the spirit of the Lord in resurrection power, even fashioning the body like unto His own raised body. When I saw this, I knew that this was the first resurrection which is about to happen and which will overtake those who did not come into their graves but were alive and remained unto His appearing. The blood did not become blood as it was once before, but it became blood that emerged FROM the swirling mass of glory, it was blood that was made from the blood of the covenant, even the blood of the living Christ who now moved by spirit in the physical frame. This change and this movement of the mass of glory that will happen only took one millisecond in time to do for the entire body to be changed and eternally glorified.

....

"The Lord then stood upon the earth in full regency of His glory and power the full measure of His person was clearly seen even by those who had passed from this world and who died in hope of the resurrection. As the Lord stood upon the earth I saw gathered before Him a little group of people. This group of people were joined with others who were of the same group who had once been alive but had died in times past and who were no longer living on the earth in bodies of flesh and blood. These all together stood before the Lord who Himself was now standing upon the earth in His splendour. The Lord then held out His arm over the heads of these who stood by Him and in the Lord's hand was a cloud of great glory. So great was this weight of glory that the brilliance of it was equalled to the brilliance of the glory of the Lord itself. The glory that He held forth in His hand and over the heads of those who stood before Him was the same glory by which the Lord had now clothed Himself. What I saw was that the hand of the Lord was not in a palm up fashion, but a palm down fashion so that the glory which His hand held was able *to descend out of His hand and light upon the heads of the waiting ones. These who then were together an Army were thus brought into the very same brilliance of glory as was the Lord, the brightness was the same, the weight of glory was the same and their bodies were the same. These all became one with the Lord as His Army in the brilliance of glory and in bodies which could not die. So, it was, the Lord raised in the first resurrection these who stood by waiting, and they were glorified."*

.... *Writings from Kenneth Visscher* ....

CHAPTER 3

The Veil Lifted

Those with unveiled faces will be revealed! So Christ's glorified body will walk on the earth once again. I had a thought that when the Son of Perdition is revealed, this could align with God's timing to reveal the Sons and Daughters of God. A thought to ponder!

From Genesis to Revelations, we see a tree of life. *This is the tree in the midst of the river that flows from the throne. On either side of the river, was there the 'tree of life', which bare twelve manners of fruits, and yielded her fruit every month: and the leaves of the tree were for the healing of the nation's* [Rev 22:2]. Kenneth Visscher brought it to my attention that the leaves on the tree are the voice of Christ that is in us. That voice goes out to heal the nations. Another tree exists from Genesis to Revelations, the tree of knowledge of good and evil. That is the world and everything it represents. *I am the TRUE vine, and My Father is the keeper of the vineyard. He cuts off every branch in Me that bears no fruit, and every branch that does bear fruit, He prunes to make it even more fruitful* [John 15:1]. Give Him permission to prune your life.

We carry the fruit on the branches! Are you seeing it yet? The tree of life includes us. We are not separated. We were always part of it, but our minds could not see because we were walking through darkness. *And I am convinced that nothing can ever separate us from God's love. Neither death nor life, neither angels nor demons, neither our fears for today nor our worries about tomorrow—not even the powers of hell can separate us from God's love. No power in the sky above or in the earth below—indeed, nothing in all creation will ever be able to separate us from the love of God that is revealed in Christ Jesus our Lord* [Romans 8:31].

A woman recently described me as "My own person." This is a great compliment because it showed me no other person can influence me toward their views. I don't belong to groups - my family and a few friends who I visit are my community. People often rely on each other with co-dependency, but my dependence is on the Lord. When that process is complete in human existence, the veil can be lifted so the Lord's image can be seen. We become living vessels for His grace and Glory to move upon the earth.

Knowing Christ is alive in you is the main key. Another key is knowing why you are here on earth. Having faith and a cry from your spirit saying, "COME Lord," will reveal Him. *He who testifies to these things says, "Yes, I am coming soon." Amen. Come, Lord Jesus* [Rev 22:20] *Wait for the LORD and keep his way, and he will exalt you to inherit the land; you will look on when the wicked are cut off* [Psalm 37:34].

He who has an ear, let him hear what the Spirit says to the churches. To him who overcomes I will give to eat from the tree of life, which is in the midst of the Paradise of God [Revelation 2:7]. The tree of life is Christ in you, the hope of glory. Anything you ask shall be given to you! *And I will do whatever you ask in my name, so that the Father may be glorified in the Son* [John 14:13].

The choice is yours - the tree of life or the tree of knowledge. That serpent lives in us. We haven't come out of the tree of knowledge until you tread on the serpent's head with your heel. Repentance! *Taste and see that the LORD is good; blessed is the one who takes refuge in him* [Psalm 34:8]. The Bible didn't mention the name of that demon serpent that tempted Eve. But after looking into the demons, one is called (Astaroth); they depicted this demon as part of the unholy trinity. She began as the woman of nature, attracting people to wealth, knowledge, and luxury. Ultimately tempting 'Eve at the tree of Life'. She was mentioned 40 times in the Old Testament, luring people into evil temptations. As this demon progressed through time, she became a naked man riding an ugly beast. So, this demon is a she/he demon! Many people are confused about their gender in this age. Is it this demon?

The temptations and sins we overcome all stem back to this one event in the garden of God at the 'Tree of Life'. Our call was to overcome the tree of knowledge and the demon serpent who lives in that tree. We are spiritual beings on a natural journey, untangling the truth within our souls. If this demon can corrupt us, we will never bring heaven back to earth. Restoration of all things! Recognising the serpent that lured us away from the purity of the Deity, is when we've come back to the beginning and the end. "*I Am Alpha and Omega, The Beginning and The Ending,*" *saith the Lord, who is, and who was, and who is to come, the Almighty* [Rev 1:8].

God created the physical world. *For in Him we live and move and have our being, as also some of your own poets have said, "For we are also His offspring"* [Acts 17:28]. The omnipresence presence of God sustains us. As above, so below! *Set your affection on things above, not on things on the earth. For ye are dead, and your life is hidden with Christ in God. When Christ, who is our life, shall appear, then shall ye also appear with him in glory* [Colossians 3:1-4].

Spiritual eternal beings in a human existence - how neat is that! We look into a mirror and see our reflection. God looks into us to see His refection. We are one with the maker of heaven and earth. There is no separation. *And I am convinced that nothing can ever separate us from God's love. Neither death nor life, neither angels nor demons, neither our fears for today nor our worries about tomorrow—not even the powers of hell can separate us from God's love. No power in the sky above or in the earth below - indeed, nothing in all creation will ever be able to separate us from the love of God that is revealed in Christ Jesus our Lord* [Romans 8:38].

Sin is a transgression of God's law and ignorance. *The fool has said in his heart, there is no God. They are corrupt; they've done abominable works, there is none that doth good* [Psalm 14:1]. Hell, people experience is their own disorder they have created with their choices to break God's order. Worldly people will come under God's judgement because they will need to come out of their own self-imposed worth (pride). *The Lord is not slow in keeping his promise, as some understand slowness. Instead, he is patient with you, not wanting anyone to perish, but everyone to come to repentance* [2Peter 3:9]. The true church of Christ has already been judged. Those who rebelled against Him or those who have fallen away in Christ are under the final judgement. But that time is not yet - we are in the harvest time.

The world is showing an evil mind and other anti-Christ behaviours. *Do not conform any longer to the pattern of this world, but be transformed by the renewing of your mind. Then you will be able to test and approve what God's will is—his good, pleasing and perfect will* [Romans 12:2]. There is no escaping these last days. You will need to buck up and get on board or you will be bucked out in the last judgement. *For evil men will be cut off, but those who hope in the LORD will inherit the land. A little while, and the wicked will be no more; though you look for them, they will not be found. But the meek will inherit the land and enjoy great peace* [Psalm 37:10]. That passage says evil will be cut off, which sounds like a separation, but it's not. There is no separation between God's love. He owns the keys to heaven and hell. He may cut them off, so they come back into a right place within themselves. That's love!

People have possession of the land. Others declare the land is theirs. Yet others who will receive the land as their inheritance for being obedient to the law of God are 'the meek'. I know which team I'm on, God's team!

Recently I saw this possession of land in action. I was handed an overview from an Aboriginal community confessing that the land they had earmarked was their Sovereign land. The sovereignty of land belongs to God, not a people. Another story was of more people who were given land as a trust. But they also had taken possession of the land and moved out of their official role. We can think we are operating in God, but we take matters into prayer and then listen to the voice of man. They often call man's voice the voice of God. That's called spiritual adultery. The wrong people have possessed the land since the beginning of time. Man's mind takes over with pride and possesses what he should not possess. But this will turn as the Scripture says: *The meek inherit the land! As dead flies give perfume a bad smell, so a little folly outweighs wisdom and honour* [Ecclesiastes 10:1]. All these groups had wisdom and honour, but they operated in folly, which is the dead fly giving perfume the bad smell. Folly is representing wrongfully!

The earth is the LORD's, and everything in it, the world, and all who live in it [Psalm 24:1].

For attitudes to evolve past ownership and possessions, Our Lord Jesus Christ, the Messiah, will bring His saving grace in the outpouring of the Holy Spirit. This grace will transform man's mind and all things. *For all have sinned and fall short of the glory of God, and are justified freely by His grace through the redemption that is in Christ Jesus...* [Romans 3:23].

I have met people who do not believe in sin or evil. New Age has taught this thinking. Looking at that comment from the perfect place before Adam and Eve opened the porthole into the tree of knowledge and good and evil, I would agree with that comment. Looking at that comment from believing in faith that all things are restored, and all men are saved, I would agree with that comment. But that's not what is around us on the earth. We have wars and rumours of wars, plagues, fornication, idolatry. Man wanting his ways to rule over God's way and calling himself as a god. All evil! All sin! But the Lord God says: *Therefore, judge nothing before the time, until the Lord comes, who will both bring to light the hidden things of darkness and reveal the counsels of the hearts. Then each one's praise will come from God* [1Corinthians 4:5]. All the hidden things will come to the surface, and all will be reconciled to Our Lord Jesus Christ. Some people have said to me, "What about people who haven't heard about Jesus Christ?" *And they will preach this gospel of the kingdom in the entire world as a testimony to all nations, and then the end will come* [Matthew 24:14]. I believe all nations have had the gospel preached to them, although there might be a few left. *Judge nothing before the appointed time! For we know in part, and we prophesy in part.*

But when that which is perfect is come, then that which is in part shall be done away [1 Corinthians 13:9].

What do you think? *If a man has a hundred sheep, and one of them has gone astray and gets lost, will he not leave the ninety-nine on the mountain and go in search of the one that is lost?* [Matthew 18:12]. I had a motel complex with homeless men. That Scripture became alive one night. All men in the complex had a curfew, and one man didn't come home. The Lord pressed upon me to leave the ninety-nine and go and find the one. I found the one in hospital and his nose had been ripped off because of falling on a glass coffee table in a fight. This young man had such a reputation for being violent. The Doctors wouldn't sow his nose back on unless I was in the room. I'll remember that night forever! I brought him home, and this man gained such a respect for me as a person because nobody had ever done that for him before. He'd gone from foster home to foster home until one day the Lord brought this man to my door. He lived with us for three months as all the men did, and he received Jesus into his heart and a new direction and way of living. It's the little things that matter in life!

I wouldn't have a clue what every man gained while with me in the motel complex called 'New Beginnings', but I know what I gained. Each one of those men were the most rebellious men on planet earth, and God put a woman and my two young daughters to live with them. Not one of those men harmed us and I walked away without rebellion in me. Those men reflected their rebellion onto me; hence it had a healing effect.

I was a new believer when the Lord gave me the complex called 'New Beginnings'. The Lord uses evil for good and good for evil. Everything we do in life has a boomerang effect. It comes back upon us! *If we judge, the same measure will judge us. Do not judge, or you too will be judged. For in the same way you judge others, you will be judged, and with the measure you use, it will be measured to you. "Why do you look at the speck of sawdust in your brother's eye and pay no attention to the plank in your own eye?* [Matthew 7:2]. I love that verse, it is so confronting. I love taking the plank out of my eye. It gives me an opportunity to see people without judging. No one knows how a person arrived at being who they have become. Most of these men had an enormous event happen in their lives to thrust them out onto the streets to become homeless. Most of the time it wasn't their doing - it was just part of their journey to meet Christ. Let God be the judge! I know He goes to great lengths to bring the lost sheep home.

I saw another Scripture in that motel complex. *So, because you are lukewarm—neither hot nor cold—I am about to spit you out of my mouth* [Revelation 3:16]. These men had one thing in common: They had prayed a prayer saying, "O God help me." With that prayer, they landed on my doorstep! One night, one man wasn't taking the experience and opportunity seriously, and I witnessed God supernaturally spew this man out of 'New Beginnings'. I did nothing, it was supernatural how it happened. I learnt to never take God for granted or ever play games with Him. God can love you with His entire hand or flick you out with one finger. *He is God and He will not be mocked. Be not deceived; God is not mocked: for whatsoever a man sows, that shall he also reap* [Galatians 6:7].

I have seen many people take their salvation and not run the race. *Therefore, since we are surrounded by such a great cloud of witnesses, let us throw off everything that hinders and the sin that so easily entangles. And let us run with perseverance the race marked out for us, fixing our eyes on Jesus, the pioneer and perfecter of faith. For the joy set before Him, He endured the cross, scorning its shame, and sat down at the right hand of the throne of God. Consider Him who endured such opposition from sinners, so that you will not grow weary and lose heart* [Hebrew 12:1-3]. We are being watched! Not only by God the Father but Jesus Christ, the twenty-four elders around the throne, all our forefathers plus the angels. There is a great cloud of witnesses! Get back in the race and 'run forest run!

CHAPTER 4

In His Image

As long as we have been alive, the world has had us look at our body image. *But the Lord says we were created in His image and His likeness. So, God created man in His own image; in the image of God He created him; male and female He created them* [Genesis 1:27]. Body image and self-image can impose, which will distract us from God's image being seen. The world is concerned with the mental perception of self. God is concerned with the spiritual outworking of grace. *The wise shall inherit glory: but shame shall be the promotion of fools* [Proverbs 3:5].

Do you not know that your bodies are temples of the Holy Spirit, who is in you, whom you have received from God? You are not your own; you were bought at a price. Therefore, honour God with your bodies [1Corinthians 6:19].

Adam had the breath of life breathed into his nostrils. This breath was the Spirit of God. We are fearfully and wonderfully made according to His image. If we follow body image and self-image, we will never be satisfied. We will be like those who chase the wind! I think that's why God created us to age, so we can see chasing self-image and body image is futile. It takes the spirit of self -control to combat self-image and body image. Alignment yourself with the glorification of the body. *Therefore, I urge you, brothers and sisters, in view of God's mercy, to offer your bodies as a living sacrifice, holy and pleasing to God—this is your true and proper worship* [Romans 12:1]. *There is, therefore, now no condemnation to those who are in Christ Jesus, who do not walk according to the flesh, but according to the Spirit.*

For the law of the Spirit of life in Christ Jesus, He has made me free from the law of sin and death. For what the law could not do in that it was weak through the flesh, God did by sending His own Son in the likeness of sinful flesh, on account of sin: He condemned sin in the flesh, that the righteous requirement of the law might be fulfilled in us who do not walk according to the flesh but according to the Spirit. For those who live according to the flesh set their minds on the things of the flesh, but those who live according to the Spirit, the things of the Spirit. For to be carnally minded is death, but to be spiritually minded is life and peace. Because the carnal mind is enmity against God; for it is not subject to the law of God, nor indeed can be. So then, those who are in the flesh cannot please God [Romans 8].

But you are not in the flesh but in the Spirit if indeed the Spirit of God dwells in you. Now, if anyone does not have the Spirit of Christ, he is not His. And if Christ is in you, the body is dead because of sin, but the Spirit is life because of righteousness [Romans 8:9].

These verses say it all! I had a total eclipse as I came into these Scriptures. For years, we walk with the spirit and overcome our own flesh, thought life, and past life decisions, which created our today. These Scriptures came alive in me! It is never my image or body when the Holy Spirit lives in me. Timing and diligence will bring us to the end of ourselves if we seek Him. We are one spirit, not two. The Holy Spirit came into me years ago. Today I came into the Holy Spirit. Reversed! The crucifixion of Christ will have its full effect. *I have been crucified with Christ and I no longer live, but Christ lives in me. The life I now live in the body, I live by faith in the Son of God, who loved me and gave himself for me* [Galatians 2:20]. Until it becomes a reality, that is just a scripture. Many would say that they knew that! To become that Scripture is different! So, my image became His image, and my body became His body. We are one! The spirit of God appeared in my eyes. So, my walk became His walk. That comes in alignment with the glorification.

But if the Spirit of him that raised up Jesus from the dead dwells in you, He that raised up Christ from the dead shall also quicken your mortal bodies by His Spirit that dwelleth in you [Romans 8:11].

Therefore, brethren, we are debtors—not to the flesh, to live according to the flesh. For if you live according to the flesh you will die; but if by the Spirit you put to death the deeds of the body, you will live. For as many as are led by the Spirit of God, these are sons of God. For you did not receive the spirit of bondage again to fear, but you received the Spirit of adoption by whom we cry out, "Abba, Father." The Spirit Himself bears witness with our spirit that we are children of God, and if children, then heirs—heirs of God and joint heirs with Christ, if indeed we suffer with Him, that we may also be glorified together [Romans 8:12-17].

And we know that all things work together for good to those who love God, to those who are the called according to His purpose. For whom He foreknew, He also predestined to be conformed to the image of His Son, that He might be the firstborn among many brethren. Moreover, whom He predestined, these He also called; whom He called, these He also justified; and whom He justified, these He also glorified [Romans 8: 28-30].

What then shall we say to these things? If God is for us, who can be against us? He who did not spare His own Son, but delivered Him up for us all, how shall He not with

Him also freely give us all things? Who shall bring a charge against God's elect? It is God who justifies. Who is he who condemns? It is Christ who died, and furthermore is also risen, who is even at the right hand of God, who also makes intercession for us. Who shall separate us from the love of Christ? Shall tribulation, or distress, or persecution, or famine, or nakedness, or peril, or sword? As it is written:

For Your sake we are killed all day long;
We are accounted as sheep for the slaughter.

Yet in all these things, we are more than conquerors through Him who loved us. For I am persuaded that neither death nor life, nor angels nor principalities nor powers, nor things present nor things to come, nor height nor depth, nor any other created thing, shall be able to separate us from the love of God which is in Christ Jesus our Lord [Romans 8: 31-39].

I am the door: by me if any man enters in, he shall be saved, and shall go in and out, and find pasture [John 10:9]. This is Jesus speaking to His followers.

My sheep hear my voice, and I know them, and they follow me: And I give unto them eternal life; and they shall never perish, neither shall any man pluck them out of my hand. My Father, which gave them to me, is greater than all; and no man is able to pluck them out of my Father's hand. I and my Father are one [John 10:27-30].

These Scriptures pronounce such great promises. I couldn't say it better than they are written by our forefathers and the Spirit of God.

There is no condemnation when we walk according to the Spirit. So, if someone condemns you for something, it didn't come from Christ. We condemn ourselves most of the time. Christ came to earth in the flesh to free us from sin and death. So, death has no hold over us, nor does sin. Christ put flesh to death so the righteous requirement could fore fulfil God's law. The Spirit of Christ lives in us. The Father will give us the same power that raised Christ. That is huge! Our body is already dead because Christ lives in us. So, if the body is dead, we must be alive in Christ's body. If we can't imagine that, how can our faith expect what we can't imagine. Our bodies are dead already but the spirit is life. He will give that same life to our mortal bodies. There's the glorification in that passage! It's from the inside out! Life will come through our mortal bodies from the spirit who lives in us. The Spirit of God speaks to the spirit within our mortal bodies. Because we suffered with Christ, we will also be heirs with Christ. For us, it was overcoming our fallen nature. With Christ, it was all the sins of the world He took upon His body. We are already His reflection upon the earth; we just haven't fully identified with this truth.

Most people live their lives in the natural realm. When someone dies, we celebrate what that person did on the earth during their time. If they were a businessperson, we would say how great they were in business. A singer, performer! A writer, how many books they wrote? And so it goes! These things are storing our treasures on the earth, not in heaven. We try to prove we can do things! Some things get to continue, while other things fall. These achievements feed our pride most of the time. Our pride gets hurt when it falls, but that makes us better equipped to stand in His Glory, not our own.

What I found in producing businesses or communities is that all those things lead me to Christ's fullness.

Lay not up for yourselves treasures upon earth, where moth and rust doth corrupt, and where thieves break through and steal: But lay up for yourselves treasures in heaven, where neither moth nor rust doth corrupt, and where thieves do not break through nor steal: For where your treasure is, there will your heart be also [Matthew 6: 19-21].

If you died today, what would they say? For me, I reached what individuals achieve in the natural realm. But what I noticed was the Lord kept clearing away what I achieved under my leadership and power. He had alternative plans for me! The Lord instructed me to give up all and follow Him! The rich man asked Jesus how to enter the Kingdom of God. Jesus responded, "Give up all and follow me." The rich man couldn't do it and he walked away. I didn't walk away; I followed! There is a hope for the glorification on earth. Not all people die! Enoch, and Elisha, left the earth without tasting death.

My love for the Lord God developed into a marriage of trust and faith as He had me sleep out in the wilderness, rivers, mountain tops, and deserts. It's possible to connect to Him when you're near nature and the world fades away. I could hear Him laugh at me now and then because of something I did which to Him was funny. It opened a side of Him I enjoyed! My heart grew more in love with Him as I trusted and walked with Him each day. I have experienced the Lord for twenty-eight years, and each year I ask to know Him more. I do not store up treasures upon the earth. My treasure is the love He has shown me during the time I have spent with Him on the earth. I believe in His plan to glorify His chosen people, so I walk that path in anticipation. That amazing Holy moment when He quickens my mortal body, WOW! I keep my eyes fixed on the prize, which is Christ, the hope of my calling. It is His image I long for and it's His body I desire. It is a marriage made in heaven!

The kingdom of heaven will be comparable to ten virgins, who took their lamps and went out to meet the bridegroom. Five of them were foolish, and five were prudent. For when the foolish took their lamps, they took no oil with them. But the prudent took oil in flasks along with their lamps. Now while the bridegroom was delaying, they all got drowsy and began to sleep. But at midnight there was a shout, "Behold, the bridegroom! Come out to meet him." Then all those virgins rose and trimmed their lamps. The foolish said to the prudent, "Give us some of your oil, for our lamps are going out." But the prudent answered, "No, there will not be enough for us and you too; go instead to the dealers and buy some for yourselves." And while they were going away to make the purchase, the bridegroom came, and those who were ready went in with him to the wedding feast; and the door was shut [Matthew 25].

When You said, "*Seek My face*" my heart said to You, "*O LORD, I will seek Your face*" [Psalm 27:8]. This verse is straightforward: God requires us to pursue His face. His appearance! *Therefore, I urge you, brothers and sisters, in view of God's mercy, to offer your bodies as a living sacrifice, holy and pleasing to God—this is your true and proper worship* [Romans 12:1]. I've used that verse before in this book, and I'll use it at the end of this book. This is the major key to becoming glorified. If you desire to walk on earth in His image, you will seek His face and offering your body as a sacrifice. A good old Australian saying, 'Get over yourself'. We don't think about the importance of that saying. That saying means we are not interested in your version of the truth. It's the Spirit of God that carries the weight of Glory that propels us to listen.

When I was in business, I considered things that were out of order so I could improve and bring a new order. I was also watching the destiny of the business to determine how to extend its future. Walking with God, I apply the same knowhow to peer deep within my soul to uncover elements that are out of order. It works! I look into the future to see what God wants to do for His Kingdom on earth. With order, God can bless. He pours out His Spirit into a clean vessel. The more I removed, the more He came and filled me with Himself. We are running His race, not our own! To overcome and to shine His light takes perseverance, long suffering, and endurance. Running His race needs to be a desire and a cry from our heart. You can't win any race if you are complacent, asleep, or lukewarm. To surrender one's life and to lay our bodies down as a living sacrifice is another step. We give our self over to the one who purchased it at a price, Christ. He gave up his life for us. So, we could live conforming to His purposes. We are His image, reflection, and presence on earth. All is done!

Redeemed, Sanctified and Glorified the next stage!

Our bodies are already dead! But Christ lives in us by the Holy Spirit. The Spirit of God, who raised Jesus from the dead, lives in you. *And just as God raised Christ Jesus from the dead, He will give life to your mortal bodies by this same Spirit living within you* [Romans 8:11]. Spirit calls to spirit, deep calls to deep! He isn't talking about when our bodies go back to the ground. God is talking glorification while alive in this body on the earth. Shifting our mortal bodies to immortal is the same as Christ's body. *For this corruptible must put on incorruptible, and this mortal must put on immortality* [1 Corinthians 15:53]. The overcomer has oil in their lamp, ready for the quickening from mortal to immortal. Not all who say, "Lord, Lord" will be in this first glorification. It's those who have washed their robes!

Individuals are robbed because they have compromised themselves. 'Self' got in the way. This generally leads to complaining. Remember why the Israelites got dropped in the desert? They were whingers. They hadn't received what they desired because of their disobedience, not because the Lord was slow. That trip from Egypt to the promised land was an eleven-day journey. Forty years to cross that desert, and they still didn't get to receive. The earth opened and swallowed them up. When Moses showed them the answer to their dilemma, they ignored the answer because it meant transformation. People don't like change. Change means doing things differently. A time will happen when change will appear upon all humanity regardless of your free will. God must get saddened when He sees His children being robbed of all the best that He can give them. I know it hurts a parent to see their children robbing themselves. *There is a way that seems right to a man, but its end is the way of death* [Proverbs 14:12]. *Enter through the narrow gate. For wide is the gate and broad is the road that leads to destruction, and many enter through it* [Matthew 7:13].

Open the Ancient Paths! "This is what the Lord says: *You stand at the crossroads and look; ask for the ancient paths, ask where the good way is, and walk in it, and you will find rest for your souls* [Jeremiah 6:16]. There are ancient paths that open the portholes for heaven to come into earth. The distinguished men our forefathers, walked in them - Enoch, Elijah, Elisha, Moses, Paul, Jesus, and others unlocked heaven on earth. Their lives were the portholes to bring heaven to earth.

We are part of this realm, and anointed as they were to penetrate the ancient paths. Our fathers called down fire, commanded rain, and negotiated with God not to destroy a nation. They raised the dead and cast out demons! They made the blind see, and the sick were healed, and the lame walked. They likewise were transported across the earth at will. They made kings and kingdoms tremble at the word of the Lord. Two of these men were drawn to paradise without tasting death. There is a world living side by side with this natural realm. And that realm is in you and me! We just need to go to this spiritual realm before the natural realm devours us for the day. It is supernatural but more natural than the natural! It's the portholes and the ancient paths. *The time has come!* He said, *the kingdom of God has come near. Repent and believe the good news!* [Mark 1:15]

God gave commandments to carry us into these ancient ways. Jesus said: *Love the Lord your God with all your heart and with all your soul and with all your mind* [Matthew 22:37]. The second was: T*hou shalt love thy neighbour as thyself* [Mark 12:31]. Following these commandments with the other commandments, we see kingdoms fall, just as Moses did. Moses carried the oracles of God, which was the beginning of restoring the ancient path. Elijah and Moses appeared on the mountain with Jesus as translated beings. It's written *that Elijah will return before that great and terrible day of the Lord. And he will turn the hearts of the fathers to the children, and the hearts of the children to their fathers. Lest I come and strike the earth with a curse* [Malachi 4:6].

The supernatural spiritual realm is where physical limitations disappear. God talks of doorways, portholes, and pathways being opened before us. Angels ascend and descend from heaven. The spiritual realm comes into the physical. *Howbeit that was not first which is spiritual, but that which is natural; and afterward that which is spiritual* [1 Corinthians 15:46]. God made Adam (natural) and then He breathed life into his nostrils (Spiritual). First the natural, then the spiritual! We get unction's in the natural and bring it back into the spiritual. The answer from the spirit comes back into the physical. It's a dance between heaven (spiritual) and earth (natural) at the same time. "Thy Kingdom Come".

Once a mantle has been received upon the earth, it only needs a person to reactivate its power. Jesus Christ is the doorway; The ancient paths and mantles are not gone. *Ask and it will be given to you; seek and you will find; knock and the door will be opened to you* [Matthew 7:7]. The mantle of Elijah is still on the earth. Then Elisha asked for a double portion of the anointing that Elijah had. It was given to him in a double portion. He did exactly double the miracles that Elijah did. Jesus Christ's mantle is still here!

The mantle of glorification is on earth. Jesus brought it in! The next move of God, His people, will connect to this mantle. Jesus Christ has the oracles and keys to the ancient paths.

For the kingdom of God is not in word, but in power [1 Corinthians 4 :20]. These ancient paths won't be seen by the people who operate in demonic grids outside the doorway of Jesus Christ.

Wisdom of God! *That the God of our Lord Jesus Christ, the Father of glory, may give to you the spirit of wisdom and revelation in the knowledge of Him* [Ephesians 1:17]. *The eyes of your understanding being enlightened; that ye may know what is the hope of his calling, and what the riches of the glory of his inheritance in the saints* [Ephesians 1:18]. If we haven't received this type of wisdom, we may see the glory as a cloud. But we call to understanding to reveal that glory is power and might from on high. Solomon asked for wisdom and understanding

Because he asked for wisdom, God granted him riches and power. He developed into the most powerful King, gaining the respect of the other Kings. He wasted that wisdom and understanding by taking notice of his seven hundred wives that brought a belief in the opposite spirit [Baal, Ashtoreth, and Molech]. He allowed the worship of other gods into his kingdom so trade in business would be prominent. 'Put no other gods before the one true God.' Solomon broke many of the ten commandments. His kingdom was handed to him by King David, his father. There was a lack of appreciation that caused compromise and his downfall. There is a lot to be said about working for something opposed to this generation who are handed so much. They also have a lack of appreciation and respect growing inside them.

Today, we find many who have hardened their heart and walk in ignorance through a lack of knowledge of the Lord. They go into captivity for the same reason: lack of knowledge.

Or they move into the opposite spirit, the same as Solomon did. Listening to demon spirits who bring knowledge from the tree of good and evil. The Spirit of God is always conflicting with the spirit of this world.

The ultimate hope is to go beyond the tree of good and evil and knowledge back into the greatest union ever created by God. The reintegration of both human and divine, 'the marriage'. The bride has made herself ready for this great day awaiting her King to come. *That He might present to himself a glorious church, not having spot, or wrinkle, or any such thing; but that which is holy and without blemish* [Ephesians 5:27-29]. Glorification!

The dead tree Jesus Christ hung on represents the tree of 'Knowledge of good and evil'. We need to go through the tree to overcome ourselves! This takes us to the tomb of glorification and resurrection. Resurrection is something that was dead being brought back to life! It's a place of grief replaced with a place of glory and celebration. *To bestow on them a crown of beauty instead of ashes, the oil of joy instead of mourning, and a garment of praise instead of a spirit of despair. That they might be called trees of righteousness, the planting of the Lord, that He might be glorified* [Isaiah 61:3]. Notice they are called trees of righteousness. Not a dead tree!

We have nothing to work out in the world anymore because of God. The end of the tree of knowledge of good and evil will become visible once the overcoming process is completed. It's a porthole within our soul. When Eve took that fruit, she opened the porthole to death in her soul, and Adam followed with the rest of humanity. When Jesus hung on the cross, He took death in that porthole and placed it under His blood, His Holy blood. *This day I call the heavens and the earth as witnesses against you, that I have set before you life and death, blessings and curses. Now choose life, so that you and your children may live* [Deuteronomy 30:19]. Imagine every time you choose the tree of good and evil, you are choosing to put to death your children. Most people would never think of that because we've taught them to go out and achieve for your children's children's inheritance. This type of achieving is in the dead zone. To choose life is to choose Christ every day in every way. That's having your riches stored in heaven! *For where your treasure is, there will your heart be also* [Matthew 6:21].

As I came to the end of the tree of knowledge of good and evil, I was taken to my promised land. For years, I have held a vision of a land where heaven would touch earth, and I could build up the walls and ruins so the Lord would have a dwelling place upon the earth. Build my house, and I will build your house. This is what the LORD says: *Heaven is my throne, and the earth is my footstool. Where is the house you will build for me? Where will my resting place be? Has not my hand made all these things, and so they came into being? declares the LORD. This is the one I esteem: he who is humble and contrite in spirit, and trembles at my word* [Isaiah 66:1-2]. The Kingdom people serving the same God with the same purpose. *The Lord says, When the LORD brought back the captivity of Zion, we were like those who dream* [Psalm 126:1]. When a gift is given from the Lord, it comes with no struggle to us. All we need to do is to adopt the skills the Lord has honed within our lives to accompany His vision with His power and might. *All things work together for good to them that love God, to them who are the called according to his purpose* [Romans 8:28].

The journey was to cross over from the desert land into the promised land. There is an end to getting there, and there is a beginning to starting a new life full of joy, laughter, and purpose in the land. Only two people from the initial thousands who crossed the desert from Egypt got to enter their promised land. *Not one of all the Lord's promises to Israel failed; everyone was fulfilled* [2 Joshua 21:45].

I will declare that your love stands firm forever, that you have established your faithfulness in heaven itself [Psalm 89:2]. Understanding it isn't your strength and vigour that is called for. It's the Lord's strength, power, and might that can and will establish His Kingdom on earth. It is the Lord's right arm and hand that will bring you into all good things.

A friend of mine is always mentioning the AA groups. Alcoholics Anonymous has a twelve-step program. The first step is to admit they are powerless over their ways and that their lives have become unmanageable. That's where humanity is right now! The next step is to come to believe that a power greater than ourselves could restore us to sanity. The third step - decide to turn our will and our lives over to the care of God.

Since the birth of time, the world has had smoke and mirrors built up through the treachery of lies. It's been impossible to reflect Christ's glory in the old wineskin or the world. But it hasn't been time to show His glory. When you reflect truth, they deflect truth, and the accuser of the brethren steps in. *And I heard a loud voice saying in Heaven, now have come salvation and strength, and the Kingdom of our God, and the power of His Christ; for the accuser of our brethren is cast down, who accused them before our God day and night* [Revelations 12:10]. The accuser functions by implanting a lie in the heart of everything. Wars come from this spirit, broken marriages, murders, and the list is lengthy. I have noticed people believing the untrusted source and calling this their trusted source. This is the spirit that entered at the tree back in the garden. Adam blamed God for giving him the woman. This accuser needs to be locked up in the abyss for 1000 years. To have a different result is going to take more than our power. We can see the accuser if we open our eyes to our understanding.

The accuser has bombarded our minds with a dreadful story of mankind. Our image, age, and death follow this spirit. We believe the lie because we've been in it for too long. Our minds need the transformation into God's truth. We are glorified beings. That is the truth! The outpouring of the Holy Spirit can open eyes, and that's the call of my heart. *And it shall come to pass in the last days, saith God, I will pour out of my Spirit upon all flesh: and your sons and your daughters shall prophesy, and your young men shall see visions, and your old men shall dream dreams* [Acts 2:17]. When this outpouring happens, there will be no stopping the Kingdoms, power, and Glory being seen - on earth, and upon people who have overcome.

That's when, *the LORD will open the heavens, the storehouse of his bounty, to send rain on your land in season and to bless all the work of your hands. You will lend to many nations but will borrow from none. The LORD will make you the head, not the tail* [Deuteronomy 28].

Only a few arrive at the promise land in history! The Lord gets excited when His people arrive. When I arrived, I felt

His excitement. The Promised Land is your book written from heaven coming alive on earth. It's the divine marriage! We have waited for this moment, and He has cheered us on to complete the race. Often, our excitement is for ourselves. Because we see our future and dreams come alive in one moment. But today I saw that excitement in the Lord's eyes. He has been waiting because it's His plan and His future, not just ours. We are partners. The Bride and Bridegroom are one flesh, one dream, one life.

We will repeatedly fall short of developing into who the Father appointed us to be if we are waiting for humanity's approval. Knowing without a doubt that you are where the Lord has planted you, that's adequate knowledge. Don't stare into the eyes of humans for consent. *The Lord will bring you into a good place! The LORD is my chosen portion and my cup; You have made my lot secure. The lines have fallen to me in pleasant places; Yes, I have a good inheritance* [Psalm 16:6]. When the Lord gives you a gift, there is no need to beg, convince, or struggle to take that gift on in your own strength. When a gift is presented, all we do is thank God. *Rejoice always, pray continually, give thanks in all circumstances; for this is God's will for you in Christ Jesus* [1 Thessalonians 5].

There's a curse that needs to be reversed. That curse came over Eve and was passed down throughout all generations. *To the woman, He said, I will make your pains in childbearing very severe; with painful labour, you will give birth to children. Your desire will be for your husband, and he will rule over you.* [Genesis 3 :16]. This glass ceiling woman is this curse. It grows from the tree of knowledge of good and evil. God pronounced the curse upon women. It was our consequence for taking the forbidden fruit.

Women had been ruled by men until one day they pushed back and pushed men out of their position. Push, pull and control between men and women is how we are nowadays. The result would be different if we handled things of the flesh in the Spirit. Our soul's connection to evil will be discharged if we reach the place of renouncement of the evil tree. Petitioning God to restore us! We can walk in His garden again if we open the ancient gates of the tree of life. Remember, we cannot walk in this garden because God has angels guarding the gate. *He drove the man out of the garden! God placed the cherubim and a flaming sword that turned every way to guard the way to the tree of life.* [Genesis 3:24]. Conquering our fallen Adamic soul back to the very spot that is being spoken about in this passage is where our identity was hidden. We can be restored as glorified beings. This is our hope! To walk in the garden once again is the promise. It would reverse the curse that was on women. The toil of the land would be reversed off all men.

Stay alert! Watch out for your great enemy, the devil. He prowls around like a roaring lion, looking for someone to devour [1 Peter 5:8]. Evil knows you are about to bring something to earth that will supersede all things. He will try to prevent you if he can. The Leviathan spirit is the spirit of pride. This spirit has been on earth since Satan was dropped to the earth. It's part of the tree of knowledge of good and evil. It takes the truth and twists it like a crocodile rolling in the water. Its job is to break contracts such as marriage vows, bring division, and constantly twist the truth. It establishes itself as a false god and demands we must stand with him in the fallen tree. This is pride! Fire was in my eyes as I pulled down the stronghold that this spirit has had over our families, nations, and promises. If we are going to get back what was stolen, we need to go all the way. *But if he is found, he shall restore sevenfold; he shall give all the substance of his house* [Proverb 6:31]. Claim what legitimately belongs to Jesus Christ seven-fold and that also belongs to you. You are one body with Him!

According to the Bible, the land of Canaan was the 'Promised Land' that God gave to Abraham and his descendants. We all have a Promised Land, a land of hope. A place within our being that is promised to us. That's "Thy Kingdom Come" on earth as it is in heaven. Each one of us has His plan from His Kingdom just waiting to be established on earth. Arise and shine with His plan!

When we come into our Promise Land we must remember to keep our eyes fixed on the Lord, *for I have spoken, and I will bring it to pass; I have purposed, and I will do it* [Isaiah 46:11].

Overcoming our fallen nature allows more of the Lord to come through our earthen vessel, so His glory is seen. The Lord commanded us to overcome the world. *And I heard another voice from heaven, saying, come out of her, my people, that ye be not partakers of her sins, and that ye receive not of her plagues* [Revelations 18:4]. The only person separating you from the Spirit is you. The Lord is revealed through your earthen vessel. *But we all, with unveiled face, beholding as in a mirror the glory of the Lord, are being transformed into the same image from glory to glory, just as from the Lord, the Spirit* [2 Corinthians 3:18].

The world has never seen a harvest of this magnitude that is about to take place. The Glory is here on earth! We will see Christ when the veil is removed from those who are set aside. There is a Scripture that speaks of the gathering in the air.

This is when the last trumpet blows. That's before the great wrath of God is about to come upon the earth. It's further down the track from the present day of 2022. It is the second gathering. Two major happenings are spoken about. Those who overcame will be the first to display His Glory. The second is for everyone who washed their robes at the trumpet call.

Many sermons over the years have missed this truth. I could see that the teaching was an escapism teaching that put us all gathered in the air. Sorry to disappoint but that isn't the truth. We have a harvest to bring in. The witnesses who will appear in the last days have been misinterpreted as well. I'll save that for another time - that's an interesting study!

Therefore, take up the full armour of God, so that when the day of evil comes, you will stand your ground, and having done everything, to stand [Ephesians 6:3]. This armour is His glory! *He will cover you with his feathers, and under his wings you will find refuge; his faithfulness will be your shield and rampart* [Psalm 91:4]. When we overcome, we become His Glory, and we stand covered under His wings. Protected by evil. Oneness! Evil can't touch us if we have no darkness within our souls. It has no permission or authority. *Be perfect, therefore, as your heavenly Father is perfect* [Matthew 5:48]. It's possible if it is written! Many preachers have declared it isn't possible to be perfect on this side of the grave. I have never believed that! Jesus Christ was perfect, and God the Father said to be perfect. It's possible! Abraham was also told to be perfect. It is our job to test everything! *Test all things; hold fast what is good* [1 Thessalonians 5:21].

CHAPTER 5

Bringing Heaven to Earth

Moving into your calling or vision upon the earth! Leadership of any vision comes down to an orchestra of players and a conductor. The conductor knows the order; The players know when to play their notes. The song, sound, and notes came from the arrangement of music, which is spirit. Before each player goes to the orchestra, they have been trained in their roles. The conductor also knows their role and can allow the sound of the music to become one sound with many pieces. The sound travels and breaks open what needs to be opened. The most important part is to allow the freedom of the music to go out without ownership. We were just privileged to be part of the orchestra. The people who have been asked to play the music are grateful for the opportunity. Hence that is oneness! *For as the body is one, and hath many members, and all the members of that one body, being many, are one body: so also, is Christ* [1 Corinthians 12:12].

Any leftover fears will surface when you move into your calling. I saw 'spiritual adultery'. Man's will deferring to man's will - that's spiritual adultery! That curse makes people get into positions they shouldn't be in. We see an entire world being run in spiritual adultery. The world nowadays is no better than Sodom and Gomorrah, and you know what God did to that place! The beginning from the end is known by Him who will transform this Sodom world into His Kingdom. Christ's Kingdom on the earth is the restoration of all things.

The people who reign with Christ need to break the decree

from the land. A decree is 'an official order that has the force of law'. If these decrees are not broken, we will stand no chance of seeing His Kingdom being established upon the earth. With this type of faith, we are expecting the impossible to become possible. *Now faith is the substance of things hoped for, the evidence of things not seen* [Hebrews 11:1]. The angel went to her and said, *Greetings, you who are highly favoured! The Lord is with you* [Luke 1:28]. The Lord is with you, so be assured of things hoped for. This brings His Kingdom to the earth with the authority He has invested in you.

When the angel told Mary, she was carrying the King of Glory, she was reassured of things to come. You would never believe in a million years, the Lord would have Mary give birth in a stable, but He did. It didn't look like she was well-favoured. But she was! The King ordered the killing of all the male children under the age of two. That's a decree! He knew the King of Glory was amongst them. They hid Jesus from this order of killings; hence, God will do what is right in His eyes, not our own!

When you walk with the Lord, things hoped for don't always look like they will match up with our vision. Often the contradiction will present itself alongside the blessing. The aim is to be assured and trust that the Lord is more than able to bring His vision into reality. *Now to him who is able to do immeasurably more than all we ask or imagine, according to his power that is at work within us* [Ephesians 3:20]. Praise opens the heavens and pours out the blessing. A thankful heart is what's required. *I will open the windows of heaven for you. I will pour out a blessing so great you won't have enough room to take it in!* [Malachi 3:10]. Praise and thanksgivings open heaven.

Remember, in all the opportunities we are offered, it's His Glory needing to be seen, not our effort. So, the earth becomes His footstool is our journey and call. Thus saith the Lord, *the heaven is my throne, and the earth is my footstool: where is the house that ye build unto me? And where is the place of my rest?* [Isaiah 66:1]. "Thy Kingdom Come"!

We must have boldness in who we become in order to harvest souls and establish God's Kingdom. We become coheirs with the Spirit and take back what has been stolen! To see the restoration of all things. *Herein is our love made perfect, that we may have boldness in the day of judgment: because as He is, so are we in this world. There is no fear in love; but perfect love cast out fear: because fear has torment. He that fears is not made perfect in love. We love him, because he first loved us.* [1 John4:19].

God gives individuals who are in wrongful positions the chance to return to their rightful place. When they protest, He steps in and reclaims what they have robbed. *The earth is the LORD's, and everything in it, the world, and all who live in it* [Psalm 24:1]. Breaking the decrees allows God to turn the tables away from our enemies into our favour. *For to the one who pleases God has given wisdom and knowledge and joy. But to the sinner, He has given the business of gathering and collecting, only to give to one who pleases God. This also is vanity and a striving after wind* [Ecclesiastic 2:26].

We need to learn how heaven operates to complete our story. Curses are a true phenomenon - they need to be destroyed. It's another key to break through into the promises of full restoration. Curses will halt the flood of favour in our lives, or opportunities will not flourish. *The Lord has taken away*

His judgments against you. He has cleared away your enemies. The King of Israel, the Lord, is in your midst; You will fear disaster no more [Zephaniah 3:15]. We have only one adversary, but many workers for that enemy. Our carnal nature is where they live! The iniquities of our fathers go down generations, all the way back to Adam and the decrees they spoke over our land. When we were born on the earth, we instantaneously inherit our forefathers' iniquities.

The world is experiencing disasters! Death and destruction have been a part of the culture for generations. Visions or dreams of our destiny seem to continually not come to pass because destruction comes and disrupts the plan from developing into existence. We have to learn how to enter the courts of heaven. This spot is before the King of Glory. A gracious place where you receive the King's blessing to declare before His throne of grace our freedoms that Christ gave us and our rights as citizens of heaven. Remember, all curses were annulled at the cross of Jesus Christ. "All is done" were the prominent words declared on that day.

In my relationship with the Lord, I know He likes us coming before Him. It teaches us how to sit in our heavenly seat. *And God raised us up with Christ and seated us with him in the heavenly realms in Christ Jesus* [Ephesians 2:6]. It's up to us to extend into those courts and confess transgressions and iniquities of our bloodline - petitioning the Lord to reverse the decrees and curses. And lifting words of condemnation and judgement is just the start of being restored to your rightful place upon this earth. Robert Henderson writes books that cover the Courts of Heaven. He has got an excellent overview of this realm. He is a man who has overcome and knows the power of darkness that can still stand in his way when bringing heaven to earth. You will learn a lot by reading some of his books.

To draw a vision into a natural realm beyond our inner faith dimension leads us to stand in thanksgiving before the King of Glory. God's timing is often different from our timing. But we need to trust and remain in hope. *For I know the plans I have for you, declares the LORD, plans to prosper you and not to harm you, plans to give you hope and a future* [Jeremiah 29:11].

They talk of walking on the moon! Our walk on earth is more important than a moonwalk. We are called to be conquers for our eternal purpose. During my worship time, I entered a place in the Spirit realm where I felt my earthly natural body fall aside. My body rose out of the tomb of death with Our Lord Jesus Christ. Jesus drew me to the throne room and introduced me to the Father of Heaven. That's when I recognised the overcoming process has heavenly gratifications. *To him who overcomes, I will give to eat from the tree of life, which is amid the Paradise of God* [Revelations 2:7]. *To the one who is victorious, I will give the right to sit with me on my throne, just as I was victorious and sat down with my Father on his throne* [Revelations 3:21]. Standing with the King of Kings and the Lord of Lords, I was summoned to accept a seat in the heavenlies. The seat was to govern. *And if we are children, then we are heirs: heirs of God and co-heirs with Christ—if indeed we suffer with Him, so that we may also be glorified with Him* [2 Timothy 2:12]. Where your treasure is, that's where your heart is! My experience was better than the moonwalk.

Prayers are needed to determine what restrictions are on the interior of the plan. *Dead flies putrefy the perfumer's ointment* and cause it to give off a foul odour; So, does a little folly to one respected for wisdom and honour [Ecclesiastes 10:1]. I received this Scripture for an opportunity that came into my life. It conveys to me there is someone in the plan smelling up the opportunity. Intercessory prayer to the Father can remove this. Esther went before the Father, the king extended the gold sceptre toward Esther, and she arose and stood before the king. *If it pleases the king, she said, and if I have found favour in his sight, and the matter seems proper to the king, and I am pleasing in your sight. May an order be written to revoke the letters against my people* [Esther 8:4-5]. This is the place we stand in the courts of heaven before the Father. If you have been given your seat to reign, rule, and govern this land, then use it as Esther did. Eliminate the dead fly from the ointment and revoke any letters that are against you from receiving our inheritance, which is the Lord's inheritance.

After old decrees are broken, a new thing needs to be declared. *'On that day', declares the Lord Almighty,' I will take you, my servant Zerubbabel', declares the Lord,' and I will make you like my signet ring, for I have chosen you,' declares the Lord Almighty'* [Haggai 2:23]. If you know with no doubt you are chosen, then declare the new thing. *Thou shalt also decree a thing, and it shall be established unto thee: and the light shall shine upon thy ways* [Job 22:28]. To 'declare' is to state (out loud) a fact; to 'decree' is to issue an authoritative command. That's where we are walking in our new seat in heaven. We are requesting the King to extend His sceptre towards us so we can express and declare the new things. He then seals it with His signet ring and it shall be established. He will shine a light on your path! It is no longer under the authority of the fallen tree. New is here; the old is gone. We are the now and future authority, and we are the governing bodies on earth as it is in heaven, 'His Kingdom is here'. This new thing we are doing is bringing His Kingdom into the world. *No one sews a patch of unshrunk cloth on an old garment. If he does, the new piece will pull away from the old, and a worse tear will result* [Mark 2:21].

Every vision requires us to accept outcomes that are different from what we want to hear. I have learned to accept everything and bless everything. *Love bears all things, believes all things, hopes all things, endures all things. Love never fails!* [1 Corinthians 13:7]. The Lord can turn the tables in every vision. If it came from the Father, He will glorify the vision. *For I know the plans I have for you, declares the Lord, plans to prosper you and not to harm you, plans to give you hope and a future* [Jeremiah 29:11]. Commit to the Lord what you've worked out so far within the opportunity and lay it at His feet. A God-given opportunity is not done from your power and might, it's from God's grace and Glory. Wait to see what the Lord does! Knowing you are loved by Him, and you are His special possession. It may not feel so good giving up what you've identified as your destiny, but in the long run, you only want what the King of Glory wants. *Not my will Lord, but your will be done! I can do nothing on my own. As I hear, I judge, and my judgment is just, because I seek not my own will but the will of Him who sent me* [John 5:30].

Releasing opportunities into God's hands leads to the power, grace, and Glory that is required for God to be seen. It's a partnership but His glory. As it is in heaven, let His will be done here. *"Our Father in heaven, hallowed be your name. Your kingdom will come, your will be done, on earth as it is in heaven. Give us this day our daily bread, and forgive us our debts, as we* also have forgiven our debtors. And lead us not into temptation but deliver us from evil. For thine is the kingdom, the power, and the glory, forever and ever Amen" [Matthew 6:10].

If you haven't got this fight to take back your future and inheritance, then you're just going to sit in your ordinary until you die! My wall is looking like a movie I've seen, 'A beautiful mind' with Russell Crow. I write the steps that God asks us to take so I can follow His description to His Glory. If you don't have a vision for His Glory, you will never see it.

To take back all that belongs to the Lord out of the hands of those who have controlled the population is the mission we embark on daily. These unholy people are serving death, not life! I call for the winds of God from the four corners of the earth to blow and shake the tree of good and evil. *I will bring the four winds against Elam from the four corners of the heavens, and I will scatter them to all these winds. There will not be a nation to which Elam's exiles will not go* [Jeremiah 49:36]. They portray Elam as a nation which must drink the cup of God's wrath. A nation is a people who think they are in charge, but they are not. We can't continue with this charade knowing that death is holding the reign on earth. I won't allow this to happen anymore because it's not the correct order. You may say, who are you to think you can change anything? I would say, it isn't me who will change things. It is a people who have partnered with the Father in heaven, saying that enough is enough. We, the people of Christ, have had enough. Give back seven-fold what has been stolen!

It's the year of Jubilee, August 2022. Jubilee in Hebrew is the year at the end of the seven cycles of shmita (Sabbatical years). According to biblical regulations, this had a significant impact on the ownership and management of land. Israel is meant to conscientiously represent God by how they live as a community. This is what the law requires. The land can be found with love, justice, and worship. It's not Israel itself; it's a representation of a people and His Kingdom on earth.

I'm looking forward to this take back of our nations and land. With a new sign, 'UNDER NEW MANAGEMENT' - Kingdom Management!

Why do the nations conspire and the peoples plot in vain? The kings of the earth rise up and the rulers band together against the LORD and against his anointed, saying, "Let us break their chains and throw off their shackles." The One enthroned in heaven laughs; the Lord scoffs at them. He rebukes them in his anger and terrifies them in his wrath, saying, "I have installed my king on Zion, my holy mountain." Ask me, and I will make the nations your inheritance, the ends of the earth your possession. You will break them with an iron sceptre; You will break them to pieces like pottery" [Psalm 2].

We carry this weight and authority to rule with an iron sceptre. To set up and pull-down empires that have been set up against the Lord. Our position of authority to restore the world's rulership into Kingdom leadership. It's our assurance and appointment with The Father and Jesus Christ to reign and rule this world with Him. It is our duty as kingdom people to restore everything back to Him. Every time we take that sceptre in our hand and decree His Kingdom, angels follow. A fight and a re-establishing of authority, management, and ownership is transferred, spiritually and physically. When we own the nations, it belongs to the King of the Nations, Jesus Christ.

The further I walk with God, the more time I spend in His presence in the heavenly realm. It's naturally natural to be with God, then it is to be in the earthy body. To bring heaven into the earthly realm is the greatest calling we have. Otherwise, we are doing jobs on earth or finding something to do for the day. I would prefer to be open to what God wants to be done in the day. That progresses His Kingdom on the earth.

Memory Lane

Our Country of Australia was founded by the British. Our early convict ships entered in 1778. We established Australia as a penal colony. The soldiers were given orders, which they carried out. When they got to our sands, they were startled by what they found: Aboriginal people. So they did what other soldiers have done throughout history: they took the land into their own hands by murdering, imprisonment, or banishment of these people. This caused great division in this land.

Governor Lachlan Macquarie showed up to turn this country from a penal colony into settlement. He accomplished this by preparing blueprints for a township, Sydney town. He asked the British Government for money to build a hospital in Macquarie St, Sydney. The British Government refused! Hence, a rum trade with convicts and freshly discharged convicts was formed.

We haven't come that far in this story, but we see the bottom line of this country - the division between Aboriginals and white settlers emerged. Today we have Aboriginal people claiming it's their land. I understand where they are coming from, but the first settlers were stolen from as well. Our homeland was stolen, and we ended up here - Australia! We also see why people in this country drink so much. Rum was the trade because the government didn't give money. We also see abuse of people who stole a piece of bread to feed themselves or their families and were sent to a new undeveloped place by the Governing body of Britain.

244 years later!

We see a people drinking so much that when it was locked down, drinking was an essential service. If the Government hadn't allowed drinking, we would have had anarchy. Why? Because we are an abused people who can't operate without a drink in our hands.

Today we have the Aboriginals demanding separate birthing clinics at the value of 23 million per clinic all over this country. They declare the white folk are still prejudiced. This isn't true! We aren't allowed to mention black, white or primrose in our Nation. A few years back, the white folk said, "Sorry" for what they did to the Aboriginals when our ancestors first landed. They're using this "Sorry" to claim land, houses, cars, welfare, and anything else that the government will give them. The Aboriginals are looked after better than most people who live here in Australia. The Aussies have a great saying which I will use here, "Get over it." We had to as convicts! Our country portrays division between Aboriginals, and our flag the voice of governmental authorities and its people. When Covid hit, I thought we had gone back to a penal colony, not a free settlement. I don't think we have progressed as a nation, we just built on the old ways!

A new vision for our earth and our land is needed. Something different beyond our old ways. Healing for the land and the minds within the land! This new way of living is beyond man wanting to be in control. It is God who is in control of people who have overcome their abuse, ownership, control, and possessions. There is no difference between black and white; it is just a group of people coming together for the glory of

God. Look at where you stand in this picture. Let go of the old ways. You will not see the new by looking at the old. By looking into God, you will see new.

I live in a township in Australia where there is no division. You don't acknowledge if someone is Aboriginal or a westerner. We communicate with one another as individuals, not as a race. We don't care what flag you fly as long as you like it. This township possesses hospitality beyond their abuse, possessions, and thinking. It's rare! I've lived in most towns in our country, but to find "Welcome" written on the doormat of this town was great. Why is this town different? Because the Aboriginals wrote across the earth in this town "Welcome" and so it became. They have written over all the land in Australia because they were here first.

No less than three hundred kilometres out from this township is the worst division between Aboriginals and westerners I have ever seen. The Aboriginals even broke Santa's leg one year as he came down the street because he was white. I travelled for twelve years, overcoming my soul by reading the ground and atmosphere where I stayed. This gave me the ammunition to overcome! God drew me into each place that identified with a part of my fallen nature. Once identified, prayer caused me to overcome and move on. Hence, my first book was born 'How I Overcame My Own Life'.

We cannot pour fresh vision into old wineskins. New decrees over land creates a new vision! *Otherwise, the wine will burst the skins, and both the wine and the wineskins will be ruined. No, they pour new wine into new wineskins* [Mark 2:22]. We also need to loosen the bonds of iniquity, curses, and old decrees off our lives, not just the land. Not all that is written over a land is bad, but it comes to us in layers over many generations. The yoke of bondage has held us in the old wineskin. *Come to me, all who labour and are heavy laden, and I will give you rest. Take my yoke upon you, and learn from me, for I am gentle and lowly in heart, and you will find rest for your souls. For my yoke is easy, and my burden is light* [Matthew 11 :28]

A yoke is a bar borne upon a person's shoulders, from each side of which loads were suspended, or a wooden bar or frame placed over the necks of two draft animals (usually cattle) when pulling a farm implement or a wagon. Because slaves often used yokes to carry heavy burdens, they used figuratively the yoke to represent enslavement or subjection to another person, as well as oppression and suffering. Removing or breaking the yoke signified liberation from bondage, oppression, and exploitation.

This old wineskin is heavy upon our shoulders. We need to remove this yoke!

Years ago, I left the church building. They used to preach to get outside the walls and go and preach to all the nations. So, I went! Years later you see most of these buildings are empty. It's like the old pubs with the six old men down at the end of the bar. You see these old pubs derelict and abandoned nowadays, and you also see the church buildings being sold off and people converting them as homes. This is the old wineskin! Unless you move with the new things of God, you will become the six men down the end of the bar or the six old ladies in the church. Glory lives in people's hearts, not a building. We go from Glory to Glory when we overcome our fallen nature.

Think outside the old and look into the new. God has got the new! Resurrection will not occur in an old wineskin.

Ask for a new thing to spring forth. *Behold, I will do a new thing; now it shall spring forth; shall ye not know it? I will even make a way in the wilderness, and rivers in the desert* [Isaiah 43:19].

CHAPTER 6

Manifest Presence

The Lord is about to fill His temple! Behold, *I will send my messenger, and he shall prepare the way before me: and the Lord, whom ye seek, shall suddenly come to his temple, even the messenger of the covenant, whom ye delight in: behold, he shall come, saith the LORD of hosts. But who can endure the day of His coming? And who can stand when He appears? For He is like a refiner's fire and like launderers' soap* [Malachi 3:1-2]. He will walk amongst us in a real way.

There are two ways God reveals Himself to us. First, He is Omnipresence! He is everywhere and in everything. Second, the Manifest presence when He comes and speaks to us as individuals. *My sheep, listen to my voice; I know them, and they follow me* [John 10:27]. Our faith moves God to transcend time and space to manifest Himself in creation, and you're the created in His creation. God's purpose since the beginning is to reveal Himself to us in a tangible, natural way. God transcends our physical being by the order of His divine glory.

The Son is the image of the invisible God, the firstborn over all creation. For in Him all things were created: things in heaven and on earth, visible and invisible, whether thrones or powers or rulers or authorities; all things have been created through Him and for Him. He is before all things, and in Him all things hold together. And He is the head of the body, the church; He is the beginning and the firstborn from among the dead, so that in everything He might have the supremacy. For God was pleased to have all His fullness dwell in Him, and through Him to reconcile to Himself all things, whether

things on earth or things in heaven, by making peace through His
blood, shed on the cross [Colossians 1:15-20].

There it is again - through His blood! Jesus Christ has blood
on the earth. The martyrs' blood cries out, as does Jesus
Christ's blood. So, taking that theory of decrees being written
on the earth, Jesus Christ's blood wrote on the earth, and
erased all corruption, ownership and decrees. It's His blood
that writes the new story! It's His blood that owns all things.
For every beast of the forest is mine, and the cattle upon a thousand
hills [Psalm 50:10]. All things are His, and all things will be
restored. There's a thousand-year reign on this earth still to
come. Brother will not teach brother at that time, for all will
know the Lord.

It's in response to our faith that God comes! Redemption
and sanctification are about healing and cleansing a people,
whom He could come and live with. Manifest means readily
perceived by the senses. Clear, obvious to the eye or mind.

Moses, Solomon, and Joshua all had the manifest presence
of God around them. Often it was a cloud. At Pentecost, fire
came upon the one hundred and twenty in the upper room.
These people transformed the world through the manifest
presence. What the Lord is about to do in this latter-day
church will far exceed what we have seen in the past. We will
not even remember the former church because the Lord's
presence will be supreme over all other times throughout
history.

God requires a permanent place to stay. Not just a visit! He
seeks a people whom He can abide with permanently. His

Lordship will manifest in us when we abide in His presence! Our hope and only hope is the manifest presence of our Lord. He will be seen in us and around us. *And He said to me, 'You are My servant, O Israel, In whom I will be glorified'* [Isaiah 49:3]. God reveals everything to us because we are no longer servants, but friends. And with friends, you reveal your plans. Through the people God called out and set aside, He will reveal His inner most secrets.

Continue on your journey until you see the Promise Land! That's where God wants to dwell with us. I have seen the land. I've seen my place where the presence will be when the Lord declares it is time. *But God chose the foolish things of the world to shame the wise; God chose the weak things of the world to shame the strong* [1 Corinthians 1:27]. It doesn't take the wise to do the will of the Father; it takes the foolish and weak!

Throughout history, the tabernacle was a place for God to dwell among his people. Some years after they settled into the Promised Land, King Solomon replaced this temporary structure with a larger, stationary building called the temple. Centuries later, Babylonian soldiers destroyed this temple when they took Israel away into captivity. When their captivity ended, men named Ezra and Zerubbabel led a construction project to rebuild the temple. This second temple lasted until the ministry of Jesus but was not as grand as the first temple. Centuries later King Herod renovated and expanded it on a massive, opulent scale to gain political favour with the Jews (19 BC). Several decades after Christ's earthly ministry, the Roman empire demolished it completely (AD 70).

Jesus Christ dwelt among us! This word means 'to pitch his tent' among us. When Jesus came into the world as a human being, He was God's way of dwelling with his people in a more personal, direct, and accessible way than before. Jesus himself effectively replaced the need for a tabernacle or temple. The church building or auditorium is not God's dwelling place or home. God the Father did away with the temporal by using Jesus Christ 2022 years ago to show us we are His temple, His dwelling place, and the people who will display His Glory in these last days.

We are like an ongoing building project that is continuing to grow upon the fixed foundation of Jesus Christ and the ministry of the apostles. This building project does not refer to church buildings. It refers to all of us as believers who have overcome our fallen nature. Who forms a spiritual house together for the presence of God in the world? *And anyone who does not take up his cross and follow Me is not worthy of Me. Whoever finds their life will lose it, and whoever loses their life for my sake will find it* [Matthew 10:39-40].

For a long time, we focus our prayers on going to heaven. Whom have I in heaven but You? And on earth I desire no one besides You. *My flesh and my heart may fail, but God is the strength of my heart and my portion forever* [Psalm 73:26]. Our flesh and heart need to completely surrender to the Lord, so it's not our carnal energy prayers asking or pulling heaven into earth. It is heaven being poured out onto the earth through a people who have overcome their flesh. They listen and pray according to the Spirit, so it's the Spirit of God who is praying through the earthen body. Heaven and earth working together as one! When you've become the house that the Lord dwells in, you are heaven on earth. Then you only do what you hear and see your Father in heaven doing. Jesus gave them this answer: *Very truly I tell you, the Son can do nothing by Himself; He can do only what He sees His Father doing, because whatever the Father does, the Son also does* [John 5:19]. This is moving as one body, one mind and one spirit!

Unless the LORD builds the house, the builders labour in vain. Unless the LORD watches over the city, the guards stand watch in vain. In vain you rise early and stay up late, toiling for bread to eat—for He gives sleep to His beloved... [Psalm 127:1].

God requires a spiritual habitat as glorious as when Solomon built his temple. But He calls for it in a people. When the Glory of the Lord rises upon the people, it will be visible. These dark days we're living in will call for a noticeable manifest presence of the Lord upon people who have been called. This presence will not be for all believers. The manifest presence cannot penetrate their sins, iniquities, or curses. Or any other thing that they haven't dealt with during their time of believing Jesus Christ is Lord. There are many believers in the world who just mix with the world like there is no difference between them. These people will not hold His Glory. The Glory is for those who have overcome their flesh, habits, and all shortcomings.

Today I delivered a message to a man who lives on the same 700 acres I live on. I don't talk to the man often. He is a selfish man who only wants to talk about himself, and he refuses the Lord. So, I keep my distance. A few days back, he cornered me and told me his crop of beans had not given him a harvest. Not one bean came up! The Lord gave me a word to give to him today, which you would hope will change this man forever. This is the word! *I will break down your stubborn pride and make the sky above you like iron and the ground beneath you like bronze. Your strength will be spent in vain, because your soil will not yield its crops, nor will the trees of your land yield their fruit. If you remain hostile toward me and refuse to listen to me, I will multiply your afflictions seven times over, as your sins deserve* [Leviticus 26: 19-20]. Imagine this fellow's day after that word that was written on paper was given to him? He has got afflictions like I've never seen on another human being.

He refuses to acknowledge the Lord in his stubbornness, and his crop failed. *Woe to those who don't hear the Lord! To whom shall I speak and give warning that they may hear? Behold, their ears are closed and they cannot listen. Behold, the word of the Lord has become a reproach to them; They have no delight in it* [Jeremiah 6:10]. This man is completely deaf! The surgeons operated on him and sent him stone deaf. He doesn't hear spiritually or naturally. I hope he reads the words written on paper and ponders them. I can only hope! In that same word, it says, 'I will make the sky above like iron'. This man built an observatory, so the skies are his words and world that proceed from his mouth. If he spoke in an inviting way, you may listen, but he speaks in technical terms. Unless you've been trained in the technical, you can't understand what he is saying. I have found many people don't understand the Lord's language. So nowadays I only open my mouth and speak when the Lord tells me to speak. That way I'm assured it's His voice they will hear, not mine!

Surely you will summon a nation you do not know, and nations who do not know you will run to you. For the LORD your God, the Holy One of Israel, has bestowed glory on you. Seek the LORD while he may be found; call on him while he is near [Isaiah 55:6:1]. In the final days He will display His Glory, and Kings will come to that light. But those who are rebellious and continue in their rebellion will suffer greatly. Seek Him while He can be found!

This verse says it's the Lord who will not give up until He looks at the righteous light shining out from us. *For Zion's sake will I not hold my peace, and for Jerusalem's sake I will not rest, until the righteousness thereof goes forth as brightness, and the salvation thereof as a lamp that burneth. And the Gentiles shall see thy righteousness, and all kings thy glory: and thou shalt be called by a new name, which the mouth of the Lord shall name. Thou shalt also be a crown of glory in the hand of the Lord, and a royal diadem in the hand of thy God* [Isaiah 62:1-3]. His strength, not yours! There is a fourth crown, 'the crown of glory'.

Individuals who have travelled through the fires of God will reveal His Glory. It's the purifier and refiner's fire that creates a torch in our life! They are ready to shine His light in the darkened world. It's time! Many will move to this light when these people are dressed in holiness and righteousness. *For our God is a consuming fire* [Hebrews 12:29]. This last move of God will come as fire. Nobody will escape! *Watch ye therefore, and pray always, that ye may be accounted worthy to escape all these things that shall come to pass, and to stand before the Son of Man* [Luke 21:36].

Prepare to receive the fullness of His Glory! The King is coming to His sanctuary, to His people who have been set aside for His purpose. They don't look at what is in this life for them.

They look at what the Lord wants! They are transformed and renewed by His presence. Their eyes are fixed on the prize: Jesus Christ! To become His image is to love Him above themselves. They only do what they see the Father do. They are His reflection on earth. *Arise, shine, for your light has come, and the glory of the LORD rises upon you* [Isaiah 60:1].

Holy men and women have died throughout history who reached this place of Glory within themselves. But they never got to shine in the fullness of that Glory. The Lord has reserved the hour for the latter days. I've heard of people who have been ready for decades, but are still waiting for this moment to come. The ones who have died will be raised first at the coming of Christ. Raised before the others who will be gathered in the clouds after the tribulation at the last trumpet call. There are two happenings! One now and one when the last trumpet is blown. There is a first glorification that this book and others have written, specifying the overcomers are set aside for the Lord's glory to be seen.

We, the true church, have already been judged. The darkness in the world needs to see something beyond the old wineskin. *Therefore, stay awake, for you do not know on what day your Lord is coming. But know this, that if the master of the house had known in what part of the night, the thief was coming, he would have stayed awake and would not have let his house be broken into. Therefore, you also must be ready, for the Son of Man's coming at an hour you do not expect* [Matthew 24:42]. *It shall come to pass in the latter days that the mountain of the house of the Lord shall be established as the highest of the mountains, and it shall be lifted above the hills; and peoples shall flow to it* [Micah 4:1]. *And many peoples will come and say: "Come, let us go up to the mountain of the LORD, to the house of the God of Jacob. He will teach us His ways so that we may walk in His paths." For the law will go forth from Zion, and the word of the LORD from Jerusalem...* [Isaiah 2:2].

In the last book I wrote, 'Born to be Holy', I had an attitude that I hadn't overcome regarding this very thing. I found many individuals who had been injured by religions. It was outrageous what I heard, and that same outrage dwelt in me. I considered the sanctuary the 'bee's knees! That's why I got ordained and served within the establishment. But it wasn't! It was run by humans who had just picked up theology as a major and received their authorization maintaining they could preach. There was a lot of hype, hoopla, and man reciting Scripture into a congregation without growing into that Scripture. No wonder the church buildings are empty nowadays. Their intentions may have been honorable when they commenced, but they lost the plot and started calculating how many individuals they drew into their congregation instead of loving the people in their congregation. They were in the counting house counting out the money, purchasing new lights and smoke machines - instead of investing that money on the widows and orphans. It turned into a sorry state of affairs that I couldn't apply my services to anymore. Many people I have ministered to throughout my walk had the same experience. They could see the truth! *And you shall know the truth, and the truth shall make you free* [John 8:32]. The old wine skin will be removed, and His light will shine through His people in a new way. He will correct the old wineskin, but if they refuse to move out of their religious ways, they will harden their hearts.

When Covid hit society, I noticed that many of these organisations clamoured to get on-line, so their congregations were not lost. The preacher had the thought of losing their identity. Their identity was tied up with being a preacher or leader of their congregation. That's what the Lord was trying to lose, people's identity! The Lord God allowed Covid time to come onto the earth so people would find a new way. God is in charge of all things! I hear many Christians speak that evil or Satan is in charge of the earth, but that isn't true. *The heavens are Yours, the earth also is Yours; The world and all it contains, You have founded them* [Psalm 89:11]. Humans have a free will, and we bring in darkness through our bad choices. We did this to humanity! Yes, there is Satan and demons, but it's us who bring them. *Repent ye therefore, and be converted, that your sins may be blotted out, when the times of refreshing shall come from the presence of the Lord; And he shall send Jesus Christ, which before was preached unto you: Whom the heaven must receive until the times of restitution of all things, which God has spoken by the mouth of all his holy prophets since the world began* [Acts 3:19-21].

Christ lives in us! We have the same authority to bind, tie, and loose from this earth. And our earth is our body and soul! *Truly I tell you, whatever you bind on earth will be bound in heaven, and whatever you loose on earth will be loosed in heaven* [Matthew 18:18]. It's time you started ruling this earth as it is required of us to do. God is the God of restoration! Restore everything that has been taken from you. *For I know the thoughts that I think toward you, saith the LORD, thoughts of peace, and not of evil, to give you a hope and a future* [Jeremiah 29:11].

To be who you were pre-destined to be takes a fight. To overcome the world takes a separation of identity, possession, achievements, and money. To rule with Christ requires stepping up into the seat that has been prepared. To become His Kingdom on earth takes your life so His life can live. Be who you were born to be! Don't let your life count for nothing. We only have 70-80 years to become the Glory on earth as it is in heaven. Sent to earth to become His Glory! Raise Up!

EPILOGUE

To examine our walk with Christ - *It's about being awakened by Him who created us. Therefore, it is said: "Wake up, sleeper, rise from the dead, and Christ will shine on you"* [Ephesians 5:14]. Next, we enter the overcoming process! Being healed from the inside out! Learning how God operates is unbelievable and fantastic. I have looked at our forefathers and how God operated in their lives and won battles. And it's the same as now! Faith, trust, fasting, and communion topped off with thanksgiving opens heaven and moves God's hand. The old thinking or old wineskin needs to be overcome so we can re-identify with Our Lord Jesus Christ, not ourselves. This recognition leads us to our pre-destined calls upon the earth. Pressing on, we identify the iniquities of our forefathers, curses, and decrees over our life. This generates us to break all that has been born into and spoken over us from before we were in our mother's womb. We need to decree a new thing and it will come under His Kingdom by His grace and Glory.

The vision of "Thy Kingdom Come" causes us to see with new eyes. When your flesh, thoughts, identity, and ways have been overcome, you've come out of the world. That's when you stand on Holy ground. His Spirit collides with your flesh and that's the glorification. In His time, not ours! It is said that we will be a glorified body walking on earth. There's a Scripture that says we will need to wait until our brothers and sisters come into the same place as we stand. I know people who have been waiting for the glorification for decades, others are dead. I asked one of these brothers if was he frustrated? He said no, wisdom has come to him by waiting. *And now, Father, glorify me in your presence with the glory I had with you before the world began. I've revealed Your name to those You have given Me out of the world. They were Yours; You gave them to Me, and they have kept Your word...* [John 17:5-6].

Jesus surrendered His Spirit to the Father and His flesh. The curtain in the temple was ripped in two, so we can stand in the Holy of Holies. After three days in the tomb, the Father resurrected Jesus. We don't need to die as Jesus did! But we are required to die to the world and all our fleshly desires. That brings His Glory! Picking up your perfect place in the heavenlies. Reigning and ruling with Him is the gift when you stand in the courts of heaven. To become His reflection on earth is having oil in your lamp, so when the bridegroom comes, you will be quickened with His glory to the innermost part of your being. You become one because you were always one! There is no separation from the love of God. *And I am convinced that nothing can ever separate us from God's love. Neither death nor life, neither angels nor demons, neither our fears for today nor our worries about tomorrow—not even the powers of hell can separate us from God's love. No power in the sky above or in the earth below—indeed, nothing in all creation will ever be able to separate us from the love of God that is revealed in Christ Jesus our Lord* [Romans 8:38-39]. And Christ lives in you, the hope of His glory!

Therefore, I urge you, brothers and sisters, in view of God's mercy, to offer your bodies as a living sacrifice, holy and pleasing to God—this is your true and proper worship [Romans 12:1]. The transformation into Glory lives here. When the Spirit consumes your mortal body. That's glorification, that's resurrection and that's "Thy Kingdom Come". Amen!

Continue the overcoming journey, the Promise Land exists! You are the Promise Land because you are His glory upon the earth. The vision that you hold will come into reality if you have faith and believe His processes. TRUST, FAITH, FASTING, COMMUNION, and PRAISE open the windows of heaven. They are the keys!

.... *THE END* ....

ABOUT THE AUTHOR

We were predestined before coming to earth! My walk with Christ took place when I was thirty-six years of age. I had never been to Sunday school or walked into a church, nor had I ever heard about Jesus Christ or God the Father. My encounter came with the Lord after I had lost my husband and first business. It left me with two daughters to raise by myself. I was getting back on my feet when an exceptional man appeared in my world, sprouting Jesus Christ's name. He slept in his car in my driveway for ten months, praying and opening a Bible to me night after night. I would sit with my bottle of scotch, not seeing or realising what he was speaking about. But he persisted without being obnoxious. A charismatic chap who is still my friend today! One night it was like an illuminated light fell on the words in this remarkable book called the Bible. That was my initial encounter!

The next day, I prayed my first prayer, asking Jesus Christ to save my mother. Christ presented Himself to me and spoke from heaven, audibly. I could see into the spirit realm as he stood in a doorway. He said, "Come in!" My reply was, "How do I know I can trust you?" He said, "Come!" That day I entered what would be the start of knowing the Lord on a path of faith-filled adventures. When He spoke to me, it was like rushing water, but the water had the sound of strength, mercy, grace, kindness, authority, power, love, and the list went on. A very short time later, my mother was saved!

It wasn't long before I understood the process or pathway I was required to take. It was the path of overcoming myself or my soul life. First, the spirit of God put me in a congregation to learn His word. But not all the words they spoke were correct. I had that type of personality to test the words against God's words. I became a Deacon within a large Pentecostal Church, but when I received my ordinance I handed it back and said I would find God without the walls and the roof. I wasn't very good at staying in religion! Religion didn't have the freedom I was looking for in Christ. It was restricted with whoever was holding the reins in the church and how far had they come in Christ. I wanted to go further! I wanted to follow Christ, not just learn His words.

During my first years of learning about the Father, Jesus, and the Holy Spirit, I had another encounter where the Holy Spirit hovered over my bed in a cloud. The cloud of the spirit came inside me! Soon after that encounter, I started taking homeless people into my house. I then started a motel complex for homeless men. God gave me the motel complex for $10 per week! My daughters and I lived with over seventy men coming through the doors for over fourteen months. The word the Lord gave me when I first entered the motel complex was, "Do not fear." I didn't, and we were never harmed.

After the experience with the homeless men, I started another business. It was an acting agency, a promotional agency, and I was the photographer of the actors. It was like the early business I lost, but bigger and more components. One of my daughters joined me in this business. At age 18yrs, she picked up her first million-dollar contract. Now she is an international businesswoman with awards every year. Both my daughters have matured into beautiful women and have provided me with five grandchildren.

What I'm about to describe transformed everything!

I was in my apartment in Sydney Harbour, staring out the window at the Harbour bridge and the City and I heard God speak to me, saying, "Buy a tent." I said, "Oh don't ask me to do that!" He said it again, "Buy a tent." It's the scripture of the rich man who went to Jesus and said, "How do I enter the 'Kingdom of God'?" Jesus responded, "Sell all and follow me." I know why the rich man walked away. It's a very hard thing to do. But I did it! I bought the $37 tent and gave away my identity, standing in society, occupation, income, possessions, and car. Now I said to God with a $1 in my hand, "So move me." The next thing, a relocatable van that needed to be taken to South Australia was given to me to move. A friend of mine had 15,000 acres of land with 3 km of beachfront at the bottom of Australia just before the Nullarbor Plains. He said to come here. I dropped the vehicle off, and my mate gave me another car and offered me 2000 acres of land to build what I had in my heart as a vision from the Lord, a 'village community'.

I pitched my tent, and then the mouse plague hit! Within days, my mate had found me a beach shack on the greatest escarpment where the desert meets the ocean with a mouse plague. I was a city woman without technology learning new skills of trusting the Lord. I was 40 km from the nearest person in this great expanse of sky, ocean, and desert. The spirit realm was noticeable because you have no interference from humans or technology.

The 2000 acres of land my mate gave me backfired because it wasn't a gift at all. It came with strings of control, so I gave it back. Since then, I have lived on most rivers in Australia under trees in my tent. From the city to the deserts and onto mountain tops. I had a cabin in the Snowy Mountains over the Snowy River and then into a beach shack on the beach. I've lived on boats, and the list went on for twelve years. This was the journey of overcoming myself - hence my first book was born, 'How I Overcame my Own Life'. The second book came whilst I was still on that journey called 'Born to Be Holy'.

While composing this book, I am living in a remodelled silver train carriage 76 feet long on 700 acres west of NSW Australia. I still don't have any possessions, but I do have a car. The carriage is well appointed with furniture and river water plumbed with electricity, a shower, and all the mod cons. I am at the stage in my life that I can walk away with no concern of where the Lord will take me next. The Lord spoke again and said, "You don't have to sleep near rivers in a tent anymore." What a relief because I was 63 years old when He said that!

People have asked me if I was scared on this journey? I was never fearful while out in the bush because the Lord assured me that nothing would ever harm me. The journey I had was to overcome any fear. By the time I was finished, I was fearless! Sleeping in camping grounds wasn't what I normally did. At one point, I said to the Lord that I was getting tired. It was like He turned my car on the top of a mountain into a caravan camping ground. The woman looking after this incredible place bounced out of her office like Popeye's girlfriend, Olive Oil. She said they were closing the park down because the owner had cancer. I said, "I will sleep under the tree - if you can get the owner on the phone, I will negotiate." One week later, I was inside the walls collecting the money, and everybody was coming and going through the park, but I got to stay still for a while, rest, and earn some money. It was the most spectacular place I had ever been. I was on the edge of a mountain, up 875 metres looking through a valley 80 kms to the ocean. The sun would rise in front of my eyes each morning. The presence of the Lord was more paramount there than any other place I had been. And the manifest presence of the Lord moved in on the mountain as I cleared the mountain from people who would spoil the presence. The mountain was Holy!

Beyond this caravan park, my usual sleeping place would be to find a spot in the bush by myself. I never lit a fire because I didn't want to attract anybody to me. I saw 'Wolf Creek', a scary movie about the outback of Australia and a man who stalked travellers. He would look for fires when he was stalking. That fear had me change how I did things. When it was dark, I went to sleep, and when it was light I woke up. Still, that regime followed me on the train, but I haven't got the fear anymore!

Groups or communities have not been part of my last twelve years. Even though before I left on this journey, I had very large communities and I have been the conductor of these communities. Meaning, I brought them together! It's funny that 'community village' is the vision I hold in my being, and that's what has propelled me through these twelve years. People who meet me love me, or they're surprised at what comes out of my mouth. Friends and family who have followed my journey were always willing to give me a bed for a night or a few. My daughters have families, and my grandchildren adore me. One of my daughters just bought me a beautiful convertible. There is nothing like the wind in your hair on a sunny day with the music up high, singing. My favourite moments are with my grandchildren and children. My other times, I enquire about the Lord and write what I hear or learn.

I am about to enter the real world of my dream 'community village'. Keep going is my advice to anybody who is following the Lord! Finally, dreams do come true and the hardship of the journey ends.

Then comes the GLORY!

These years of overcoming have taught me not to exalt myself. When I owned businesses, a saying of my son-in-law was, "You're a 'big wig'." It goes to your head because you achieved the life you are living, and that's pride. I had to give up everything in order to see that Christ is life. His grace is sufficient!

Today I know the Lord works out what's required to be achieved, and I move along with Him. Titles or possessions are not what I seek because they didn't make me happy when I had them. I became happy and peaceful after I overcame my own life. I have no battles in my mind, and my life is like heaven on earth! The words that come from my mouth are encased with the Lord's words, and His wisdom flows like a river from within. It was never about how much I achieved or the money I earned. Life became about walking in faith and trusting the Lord. He has shown me the way to grow into the woman He predestined. I don't conjure up the next plan. I enquire of the Lord to show me His way. It's much easier; and puts Him in charge, not me controlling my life!

I write books to see more of the Lord, not to be an author or a writer, and writing leads to exploring. I have noted with each book I write - it lifts me into knowing Him better. With this knowledge, I fall in love with Him more and more. This book is what I would hail as the glorification stage of my walk with the Lord. Many people talk about glorification, but unless you have overcome, you won't be able to display the glory in your life. When you read through these pages, you see that all of us are called, but not all have the same calling. It doesn't make one person better than another. We are all at different stages of our walk with the Lord. There is a scripture that says we will all end up with the same wages - regardless if you have been walking with the Lord for a long time or He just appeared to you.

I hope you enjoyed the book.

Love Di

www.ingramcontent.com/pod-product-compliance
Lightning Source LLC
Chambersburg PA
CBHW061107100726
47911CB00012B/444